The Sharks ~~of Hayden~~

AND OTHER STORIES

The Sharks *of* Al Jubail

AND OTHER STORIES

JOHN GIFFORD

Bowen Press

— TYLER, TEXAS —

Published 2018 by Bowen Press
Tyler, TX 75703
BowenPressBooks.com

ISBN 978-0-99947-292-7

Printed in the United States of America

For Ellen and Jackson

First say to yourself what you would be;
and then do what you have to do.

—EPICTETUS

Contents

1. What Money Won't Buy / 1

2. The Sharks of Al Jubail / 21

3. Second Chance / 39

4. Under the Bar / 65

5. Walleyed / 79

6. Confluence / 93

7. Something to Hold On To / 117

8. Trophy Water / 121

9. It Gets Under Your Skin / 133

What Money Won't Buy

It's after midnight when we finish our beer, pull on our coats, and head out the door. The cold air bites at my face, feeling like cologne after a fresh shave. We duck into Ted's Camaro. I sit in back while Marco stands beside the open passenger door.

"Hurry up and get in," Ted says. "It's freezing."

Marco says, "We got all night."

"Still," Ted says.

Marco puts the joint to his mouth and inhales. Then he climbs in and hands it to Ted.

"Hey, crack your window with that," I say.

We pull out of the parking lot and Ted offers me the joint.

"That's all right, man," I say, waving it off. "I have to work tomorrow."

Which is the truth. But it's also true that I'd rather drink myself numb than smoke my way there. We had, let's see, twelve beers at the bar. I paid for the last round, and Ted had felt obliged to leave the tip. He left a nice one, thirty percent, I think, so we can drink here next time, unquestioned about our age. We're all eighteen.

"Work?" Ted says.

"I dropped my classes," I say. "Got too much going on this semester."

"Wish I could drop one of mine," Marco says. "Sociology's eating my lunch."

"Work's eating mine," I say. "They've scheduled me early to-morrow."

"Where you work, Jefferson?" Marco asks.

"Homeland. I'm a bagger," I say.

"A bag man," he says, giggling. He takes another hit off the joint, holds it, blows it out the cracked window.

"I stock shelves, too."

"Cool."

"Not really," I say. "But it's something to do until I figure out my next move."

Snow is falling and the flakes pepper the road ahead of us as we stop at a four-way intersection at the edge of town. Other than the apartment complex across the street, there's nothing but empty fields around us. Ted pops the clutch and the Camaro comes to life, engine roaring, back end fishtailing through the intersection. He and Marco are laughing. I grab the headrest of Marco's seat and brace myself as the car goes into a spin.

The tachometer needle sweeps past 5, then 6, going from fun to asinine as it kisses the redline, climbing higher still. Smoke from the squealing tires hovers over the road, mixing with the snowflakes, which are falling like paratroopers all around us. For some reason, I think of my brother, Eddie, who joined the army last summer. He's just my brother, but ever since my dad left when I was five, Eddie's always looked out for me. He gave me some advice before he lit out for the army. "Keep a low profile," he'd said. "That'll keep you out of trouble."

That's exactly the opposite of what we're doing now as we spin in the street, tires clawing for traction, seeking purchase through the snow. Ted and Marco are laughing, leaning with the car as it flips in and out of the deserted intersection.

For a moment, I admire Eddie for leaving home, for getting out of Oklahoma and doing his own thing. Even though he joined the army, which I don't exactly understand, I still admire him. We have a picture of him on the wall at home. He's wearing his army uniform and saluting. Once, I stood there looking at his picture and, I don't know why, but I saluted him back. Then I felt like a dork, so I dropped my hand.

"Let's get out of here," I say. "We've been here too long. They're probably watching us from those apartments."

Ted ignores me. Marco just laughs, one hand on the dashboard, the other holding the joint.

All they have to do is go to class tomorrow, I tell myself. They don't have a care in the world.

Ted lets up on the gas and the Camaro finds a bit of traction as we lurch forward through the intersection. Then he punches it again and the car goes into another spin, engine roaring, tires squealing, centrifugal force making me feel like I'm in one of those rides at the state fair. Ted and Marco are still laughing. I tell myself I should've driven.

"Dude, let's get out of here before the cops show up," I say.

Now the back end comes around and we're doing counterclockwise donuts over the tire marks we just made. We hit a slick spot and the car slides to the edge of the street, off the street, into an empty field. I feel the frozen grass raking the chassis as we plow through the field, out of control. Ted's still laughing. We bounce and thrash, kicking up clumps of grass. The adrenaline is pumping through my body. I cling to the headrest, bracing myself, leaning, trying to keep from bumping my head against the window.

Then the left wheel finds a rut and the car jerks to a stop. I'm both relieved and panicked. Blue-gray exhaust hovers in the air, haunting us, as the snow continues falling, painting the ground white, reflecting the moonlight.

"We're high-centered," I say, tapping Marco's shoulder. "Let's get out and see if we can push it out of this rut."

He and Ted are still laughing.

"Come on, dude. Open the door," I say.

Ted turns the key, but nothing happens. "Car won't start," he says with a smile, as if proud of what he's done. I'm a little embarrassed for him. His parents bought him the Camaro; he has no idea how lucky he is. He's never had to drive a car that backfires, that uses more oil than gas, that may or may not start when he turns the key. He's never had to walk to school or work. And he'll never have to. I like Ted, but he doesn't get it. He doesn't get a lot of things.

"The pipes are probably buried," I say. "We're going to have to push it out of the rut."

If there's one thing I know how to do, it's getting a disabled car back on the street. Until recently, my family still lived in the country, on a dirt road. We got stuck all the time, so I've had lots of practice.

We get out of the car and assess the situation, the snow peppering our coats, the cold air numbing my nose. Our tracks in the snow tell the whole story. They're like scribbles scrawled by inept, inexperienced hands, desperate for correction and direction. Marco and Ted are still working on the joint. I tap Marco on the arm and point to the back of the car. "Let's see if we can push it out."

Despite my night of drinking, I feel very alert.

As I lean against the car's trunk, preparing to push, headlights appear out on the street. A car approaches, a black-and-white car with *Edmond Police* on the doors, snow crunching beneath its tires. It stops at the point where our tracks leave the pavement. Red and blue lights come on, flashing like hyperactive tattletales.

"Here we go," I say. "It would have to be a cop." My body is tense and rigid. For a moment, I consider running.

Now Ted throws the keys at Marco. "You were driving, dude!" he says.

"No way, man!" Marco says, backing away from the keys, which lay on the ground. He flicks what's left of the joint into the snow.

They go on, arguing about who was driving, seemingly oblivious to the cop who's walking our way.

"Gentlemen, what happened out here?" he says. Then he looks at me. "Who was driving?"

"He was," I say, pointing to Ted.

He approaches Ted and Marco. "What happened?"

I stand next to the Camaro as he interrogates them. I can't hear everything they say, but I can see by the officer's posture that he's not convinced. A few minutes later, he handcuffs both of them and walks them to the street, where another cruiser has just arrived. I follow behind, wondering if I'm going to jail tonight, wondering where I'll get bail money, wondering how I'm going to explain this to my parents.

"I wasn't driving!" Ted yells. "Leggo my arm, amigo." Then he calls to me: "Jefferson, you were driving," he says. "Tell him. You're sober."

I hold up my hands. Why would I lie? I ask myself. Why would I take the fall for something I didn't do? He's just drunk. He doesn't know what he's saying. He's just drunk and scared. He shouldn't be, though. His parents have the money to bail him out of jail. So do Marco's. They don't have anything to worry about.

If I called my mom and step-dad, and told them I'm in jail, I'm pretty sure they'd either laugh at me or tell me to stay there.

Ted and Marco are in the back seat of the second cruiser, handcuffed, squirming in their seats. I can't hear what they're saying. I'm thankful I wasn't the one behind the wheel.

Then the first officer walks over to me and I wonder if I'll be joining my friends in the police car.

"Where do you live, young man?" he says.

I think for a second, feeling irrelevant, feeling far from everyone and everything, as alone as I've ever been in this world. Then I say what I wish were true: "On the other side of town."

The snow is falling faster now, the ground hidden beneath a white blanket that's growing thicker by the minute. I'm sitting in back of the police cruiser as we drive through town. The streets are quiet and empty. A voice comes over the radio, sounding tired and indifferent.

"Up here on the left," I say, indicating the next neighborhood, where white-roofed houses peek out over a brick wall. We enter the neighborhood and follow the winding street until I tell him to stop in front of a sprawling contemporary that's all angles, edges, and glass. I pull on the handle, but it's locked. The officer gets out, comes around and opens my door.

"Thanks for the ride."

"Stay out of trouble, young man."

I walk up to the house, pretending to search my pocket for a key. Then the officer is gone and the neighborhood is silent in the falling snow. It's 1:30 a.m.

Snowflakes the size of quarters drop through the cold air, like confetti. Only there's nothing to celebrate. I head off down the sidewalk, snow crunching beneath my shoes, and go over the night's events in my mind: the fight I got into with Arl, my step-dad; going out to the bar with Ted and Marco; the car crash. With the snow falling, accumulating, numbing my senses, these seem like distant events, like they happened back in the summer. I step through the snow, passing one giant house after another, following the police cruiser's tracks out of the neighborhood. The snow is getting deeper. It distorts my sense of direction, my judgment, causing me to question every step I take.

I round the corner and stop in front of a mansion. There are no cars in the driveway, though it could easily hold six or seven. With my hands buried in my coat pockets, I try to imagine what it would be like to unlock the door and go upstairs to a warm bed. There would be lots of food in the refrigerator, a heater humming the house to sleep. For a moment, I think I hear the phone ring-ing inside, but it's only car brakes squeaking out on the street, somewhere beyond the brick wall. Then the squeaking stops and it's quiet again.

I consider going up to the house and pressing the doorbell, but decide against it. The phone will be ringing soon enough, and besides, I wasn't driving. My friend, Doug, lives just down the street. I bet I can stay with him tonight. Mom will just have to get over it. She knows Arl and I don't get along.

Three days later the snow has melted and the sting of fighting with Arl is beginning to subside, so I come back home one afternoon to find the house empty. I know Mom's at work; I don't know where Arl is. Probably out drinking. I go into my room, which, to my surprise, is just as I left it. My laundry is still on my bed, folded, and waiting to be put away.

The kitchen sink is full of dirty dishes soaking in soapy water. I heat a frozen burrito in the microwave, pour myself a Dr. Pepper, and sit and watch television, flipping through the channels and stopping when I land on a commercial for Colonel Clower's Used Cars. It gets my attention because I've passed his place on my way to work. And because I wish I had my own car. The guy in the cowboy hat says, "Your job is your credit," then he shouts out the phone number and he's gone. I get up from my chair, slide my plate into the sink with the others, and go to bed.

Sometime later, I wake to what sounds like a bowling ball crashing into my door. I open my eyes and see Arl standing there, scowling at me, breathing hard behind his handlebar mustache. He looks like an ice pick stuck into a pair of cowboy boots, and he's speaking Tavernese. I smell it.

"Where the hell you been, boy?" he asks.

"Staying away from you," I tell him as I rub the sleep out of my eyes. I know I can't stay here. I need to grab some of my things and leave. But which things?

"Well, you momma's been worried sick about you, boy. You didn't even bother to call and tell her where you was."

"She doesn't have to worry about me," I say. "I can take care of myself."

He smacks his lips and I wonder what he's going to do next. I sit up in bed, preparing myself for his charge, telling myself that if he lays a hand on me, I'm going to hit him this time. I don't care what Mom says.

He stands there, his arms swaying. Then he says, "Your brother's joined the army!"

"I know."

"They're working his ass off every day," Arl says. "Think he has time to go running all over the creation, like you? No, he doesn't. He's too busy being a soldier."

I get up from the bed, pull on a pair of jeans, a sweatshirt, and my tennis shoes. Then I grab my coat. As I put it on, Arl pokes my chest with his finger. He's taller than me, but he's as skinny as a fence post with ribs like barbed-wire strands pressing against his T-shirt. He's also cut-steer mean, but I think I could put him on the ground with one solid punch to the nose.

"Don't touch me," I tell him.

"Boy, I'm getting pretty sick of you," he says. He's got that look in his eyes, that look that says, first, he'd like to kill me, then have another drink or two. "Coming around here like you own the place. Worrying your momma."

I walk around him, open the front door, and go outside into the cold night. Arl's right behind me. I can hear his boots clomping down the driveway.

"You better keep walking, boy!" he yells. "Get the hell out my house and stay out!"

I hear his words growing distant behind me as I head down the sidewalk. I have no idea where I'm going or what I'm going to do.

A few days later, I'm hanging out with Ted and we stop by his parents' place to get something to eat. I'm off work today. I've been staying with a different friend each night, going to work in the morning, then to another friend's house in the evening. I haven't heard from my mom, but then again she doesn't know where I am or how to reach me. I'm sure she knows what's up.

We're watching television when Ted's dad walks in and asks to speak to me in private. He's an older man, much older than most of my friends' dads. He's also very calm and soft-spoken, and he's always in a suit, even at home. He leads me into his office, slides the wooden door shut and asks me if I'd like to do Ted a favor.

"I know he thinks a lot of you," he tells me. "We'd both be grateful if you'd help us out with this mess he got into last week." He adjusts his cuffs and falls silent. When he looks up, he's smiling.

"Sure, sir," I say. "What can I do to help?"

Really, what can I do? I'm just teenager trying to decide where to go next. I have a high-school diploma, a crummy job, very little money, and no car. If not for my friends, I wouldn't have anything.

"You don't have to call me sir," he says. "Call me Frank." He walks over to his desk and opens the top drawer. On the wall behind him are framed diplomas from Notre Dame and the University of Alabama. I suppose Ted will have one of these at some point, hanging on his own wall. On another wall is a photo of Frank holding a deep-sea fishing rod with a silver reel so large it reminds me of a beer keg. He's on a dock, standing beside a shark hanging from a large hook. Frank is a tall man. He must be six feet. The shark is nearly as long. "I caught that in the Bahamas," Frank says when he sees me studying the photo. "Came out of a hundred feet of water off Bimini. The guide had just started chumming the water when this thing came in. When they smell blood you can't stop them," he says with a grin. Now he holds up an envelope. "The attorney sent this form," he says. "It's an affidavit, but don't let the name scare you. It's just a statement. That's all it is. A written declaration."

"Okay," I say, although I have no idea what he's talking about, or what I'm supposed to say or do. I'm still thinking about the shark, its jaws agape, teeth exposed.

"It would just take the heat off Ted," he says, taking the paper out of the envelope and unfolding it. Then he looks at me. "And since you weren't drinking, there wouldn't be any problem. You weren't drinking that night, were you?"

"Well, I had a couple beers."

"But you can control yourself, Jefferson," Frank says. "That's the difference between you and Ted."

Actually, there are other differences, I tell myself as I glance around at the office's wood-paneled walls, the shark photo. My mouth is dry and my head is spinning.

"So, you sign the affidavit saying you were driving, and nothing happens to you because you weren't intoxicated," he says. "You weren't cited for anything, were you?"

"No."

"Of course not," he says. "You didn't do anything wrong. This certainly helps Ted. Tell you the truth, Jefferson, it would help all of us."

But I wasn't driving, I tell myself.

"Jefferson, what are you studying in school?"

Instinctively, I start to lie. "Economics," I say. But I can't lie. Frank probably already knows I dropped out. "I'm taking this semester off, though. Thinking about joining the service." This is another lie, even bigger than the first. I have no idea what I'm going to do with my life, but I'm most certainly not joining the service. It's just convenient to say. Because what else can I say? "My brother joined the army and he's got a pretty good deal. They're going to pay for his college when he gets out."

"He has my full respect, your brother," Frank says. "And I thank him for his service." He takes a seat on the corner of the desk, the affidavit in his hand. "I think the military's a great experience for a young man. Or a woman. I guess everyone can serve these days."

Not everyone, I tell myself. Not criminals. Not drug users. Not idiots. Eddie told me the military is actually very selective about the people they accept. They should be. They're protecting our country. "Were you in the service?" I ask.

Frank looks down at the floor. "No, they wouldn't have me," he says, shaking his head. "I had asthma as a child. They didn't like the sound of these lungs. It was probably just as well."

I nod my head as if I can relate, but, truthfully, I've never known anyone who has asthma. What does that even mean?

"So, Ted is planning on applying to law school some day, after graduation. This would really help him out. He'd be able to get his driver's license back, and you wouldn't be in any trouble since you weren't intoxicated."

"Yeah," I say, although the voice in my head is screaming *No! No, it can't be that simple!*

"Don't worry about the damage to the car, or anything else," Frank says. "We'll take care of all that."

"Okay," I say.

"Jefferson, why don't you take a little time and think about it," he says. "I want you to do what's right for you, but if you can see any way to help us out here, I'll sure make it worth your while."

"Okay."

"Why don't you take this affidavit home? You can look it over, or have your attorney look at it."

Ha! I think. My attorney.

There's a knock, then the door slides open. It's Laura, Frank's assistant.

"Telephone call," she says. "It's a Mister Abbot."

"Would you take a message, Laura?"

Laura slides the door shut. Frank opens a blue notebook and scribbles something. Then he tears out a piece of paper and stuffs it into the envelope, along with the affidavit, which he hands to me.

"Jefferson, just take your time and think it over," he says. "Let me know what you decide."

"All right."

On the way out of his office, he pats me on the shoulder. "Maybe one of these days, you and me and Ted can get back down to Lake Texoma for some of those stripers. I could sure stand to go fishing," he says.

"That sounds fun," I say.

On my way out the door, Ted says, "You need a ride home?" He lost his license after the accident, but somehow Frank's attorney fixed it so Ted can drive. He's driving a rental car until the Camaro is fixed.

"That's all right," I say. "I'm headed to my aunt's house. She lives a few blocks away."

Really, I just want to be alone so I can open the envelope. And once I'm out on the sidewalk, that's exactly what I do. When I see what's inside, I almost trip and fall.

My family's house is across town from where Ted lives, and it takes me almost forty-five minutes to walk there. I get tired of walking, but sometimes it's easier than asking for a ride. And it doesn't cost anything. When I get home, Mom is sitting in front of the television, filing her nails. Her hair is in curlers. I slide the envelope into my back pocket.

"You working again tonight?" I say.

"At seven," she says. "How's your day?"

I plop down on the sofa. "Fine," I say. "Where's Arl?"

"Probably finishing up for the day."

"Probably finishing off a bottle," I tell her.

She stops filing and looks at me. "I wish you wouldn't talk that way."

"It's the truth," I tell her. "You should've seen him the other night, busting into my room and waking me up. He was filthy drunk, trying to pick a fight with me. I thought I was going to have to hit him, but I left before it came to that."

Mom shakes her head and sighs, then goes back to filing. "He's under a lot of pressure at work," she says. "He's worried they're going to send his job overseas and lay him off. You shouldn't be so hard on him."

"You think I'm being hard on *him*?"

"Just try to give him a break, will you?" she says. A moment later she looks up. "You in any trouble?"

"No. Why?"

"I saw you put an envelope in your pocket."

"I got a letter from Eddie," I say. "I think I'll go read it."

"Tell me what he says."

"I will."

"Oh, I won't be home until late tonight, so you'll have to find something to eat."

I shut the door and lay down on my bed, the envelope in my hands. I take out the affidavit, unfold it, and look again at the $5,000 check. My heart is racing.

I look over the affidavit, its legal jargon, noticing the blank space at the bottom for my signature. All it takes is my signature, I think. My name. As if my name is worth anything. Evidently, it's worth $5,000.

I stuff the affidavit and check into the envelope, slide it under my pillow and close my eyes. Later, I hear the front door open and shut, and Mom driving off to work. I glance over at my door handle, wishing it had a lock. Sometime later I doze off.

Next day, I borrow Mom's Buick and drive to Colonel Clower's Used Cars, which is just down the street from the grocery store where I work. When I get out of the car, a guy in a cowboy hat, vest, and boots slinks out the door and slides down the steps. He's got his eyes on the Buick. "Time to trade, is it?" he says as he slips around the car, hands on his hips.

"It's my mom's," I say. "I'm just driving it."

"I was afraid you was gonna say that," he says. "We can't keep Buicks like this one in stock. People love them for their soft ride. They got those plush seats. Real velvety. Tickle your girlfriend's fanny. Know what I mean?" he says, grinning. Then he offers his hand. "Name's Rand."

"I'm Jefferson," I say, clamping his hand in mine and squeezing.

"Now that's a handshake," he grins. "Like a vise."

My brother, Eddie, taught me that. He said in the army, you get others' attention by shouting, or by squeezing their hands so hard they wince. "So you're not Colonel Clower?" I say.

"I wish," Rand says. "He's my boss. He's got his boots up on the desk in there. Can't pull him away from *The Price is Right*, unless *you* got a price that's right. Know what I mean? Or a Buick to sell, like your momma's here."

"I don't think she wants to trade," I say. "She likes it."

"Buick makes a fine automobile. We can't keep them in stock," he says. "What kind of car you say you was looking for?"

"That black Mustang over here," I say, pointing toward the row of cars up front. They're separated from the street by a string of fluttering yellow flags. "I've seen it the last few days, on my way to work."

"Let's go look at it," he says, "Where was it you say you work?"

"Homeland. Just down the street."

"You got a good job," he says. "That'll get you a loan around here."

"I'll probably just pay cash," I say.

"Cash money? We take that, too," Rand says. "The colonel loves cash."

"He a real colonel?" I say. "A full-bird colonel?"

"Oh, no," he says. "Colonel's his name," he says. Then, "Your dad in the army?"

"My brother."

"Thought so," Rand says. "Most people don't know one colonel from the next. He-he! Long as their chicken's cooked right, that's all they care about! He-he!"

Then, just before we reach the car, he stops me. "Hold on now. How long you say you been driving?"

"Two years," I tell him. "I'm eighteen."

He looks over at the Mustang and shakes his head. "I don't know," he says. "Most people with only two years of driving under their skin don't have the skill to handle a car that dad-blamed fast. She's got three hundred ponies under the hood, a short-throw shifter, five on the floor." He nudges me with his elbow. "See them big meats in back. This baby'll spin them like your momma's cake mixer. Yes, sir, you can burn up the blacktop in this thing."

My mind flashes to the night Ted crashed his Camaro. "Has it been wrecked?"

"No, it hasn't. I want you to look at that paint," he says. "Almost like new."

"How much is it?" I say.

Rand goes to the front of the car, looks at the windshield and says, "Eighty-five hundred. How much you say you was looking to spend?"

"Not that much," I say, opening the door and peering inside. The car smells like artificial vanilla, and I notice it has an after-market stereo system, a Pioneer. "I was wanting to stay around five thousand."

"I don't think the colonel will come down quite that much," Rand says. "We got too much into this one. She's only got ninety thousand on her. Got new tires and brakes. Just been detailed, too."

I try to picture myself driving the Mustang to work, and cruising it around town in the evenings. The thought of having my own car is intoxicating.

"It's a nice car," I say, "but it's too much money."

"Haven't you heard?" Rand says as he kicks one of the tires. "You don't need no money to buy a car. You just need a signature."

"A loan, you mean?"

"Welcome to America," he says. "All you gotta do is put your name on the paper and drive it off the lot. I bet you'd turn some heads cruising this thing down the strip on a Friday night. I think it fits you. You got some spit and fire in you. I think this is your car."

Every once in a while, when Mom has the night off, she makes a hot dinner and we all sit down to eat. Now that Eddie's left home, it's just the three of us. I don't like it, but I know it makes my mom happy, so I try to suck it up for fifteen or twenty minutes while I eat and listen to Arl ramble about his job or politics, or the new medication his doctor has him on. He's not supposed to drink while he's taking it, which has given him something else to complain about.

The evening news is on in the living room. There's a segment about city police busting a ring of copper thieves. This gets Arl's attention.

"Probably a bunch of punk kids with no supervision," he says, looking at me. "That's what happens when they have too much time on their hands, not enough to do. You know what they say about idle hands?"

I don't know and I don't care. So I take my plate into the kitchen and set it in the sink with the others.

"Thanks for dinner, Mom," I say. I give her a hug. She smiles and pats my arm, her eyes still focused on the television.

I go into my room and shut the door. Then I slide my hand beneath my pillow and remove the affidavit and check. It seems like such an easy thing to do, to sign your name and collect your money and go on with your life. But what keeps stopping me is the fact that it's a lie. I wasn't driving, so why would I say I was? And why would I put it in writing?

Because you'll earn five thousand dollars! That's why, I tell myself. You can buy a car!

I lay back on my bed, cross my arms behind my head and stare up at the ceiling, listening to Mom clearing the table, to

Arl flipping through the channels on TV. And I think about that Mustang.

Hours later, long after dark, I'm still awake, trying to work up the courage—or is it something else? Indifference, maybe—to sign the affidavit, slip it into an envelope, and drop it into the mailbox. Sign and drive.

For a moment, I wonder what Eddie would do. But I already know what he'd do. He's already done it by leaving home and joining the army.

I get up out of bed, flick on the light, and address an envelope to Frank. Then I take the check from my pocket, tear it in half and stuff it into the envelope.

I wasn't driving, I tell myself. I wasn't driving.

The cold air bites at my nose as I walk out to the mailbox, drop the envelope inside and raise the flag. Then, for some reason, I click my heels together and stand at attention, like Eddie does. And I salute the mailbox flag. I don't know what else to do.

2

The Sharks of Al Jubail

You could always tell who was winning the spades game going on across the hooch. The man with the loudest "Bite me!" was the one who'd take the pot. I never played. I didn't care for cards and couldn't stand losing my money, so in the afternoons, when I wasn't working or exercising, or writing letters to my girl, I'd stretch out on my cot and listen to the guys across the hooch risking their paychecks in the spades game. It was a small luxury, this free time, a way to relax and clear my mind. Lying there, I'd think about home and getting out of the service someday, and maybe going to college. This is exactly what I was doing one hot afternoon when my buddy, Steele, walked into the hooch with his M-16 rifle slung across his shoulder and a fishing rod in his hand. He was sweating and breathing hard, like he'd just run a few miles. He was also grinning.

Like myself, Steele was a lance corporal, an E-3, a lowly nonrate. But unlike me, he didn't seem to care. I was always thinking about the next promotion, as more rank on my collar meant more money in my pocket. Steele couldn't have cared less. I think he joined the Marines to see the world and have a good time. As far as I could tell, he had no plans for his life beyond getting through the war, getting back home to Florida, and getting laid as soon as possible. He'd brought his fishing pole because, well, he couldn't bring his surfboard. And there were lots of fish in the Persian Gulf, even if they were sharks.

Now I remembered that I needed to clean my rifle. So I sat up, grabbed my weapon, and removed the cleaning kit from the stock. "How's the fishing?" I said.

"I hooked one, but it broke me off," Steele said. He leaned the fishing rod against the wall and stretched out on his cot, his arms crossed behind his head, his rifle beside him. We'd been at the Persian Gulf port city of Al Jubail, in Saudi Arabia, for several weeks, awaiting orders to move north. And aside from standing guard duty and accompanying the Coast Guard on harbor patrols, we had lots of free time on our hands. Most guys played spades. Some, like me, lifted weights or jogged. Steele liked to fish. He *loved* to fish. Somehow, he'd managed to fit a rod and tackle box into his sea bag. Even more amazing was the fact that the graphite stick hadn't broken on the trip over from the States. "A good one, it felt like," he said.

"Too bad you can't take that fishing pole when you're out on the Zodiac," I said. "You could drop your bait in the water behind the boat and troll for sharks."

Steele sat up and swung his feet onto the floor. "That's not a bad idea," he said. Then he jammed a cigarette between his lips and lit it.

"I was just kidding," I said. "You know the captain would have your ass."

"It can be done," he said, exhaling a stream of smoke. "You watch. I'm going to catch a shark."

"The captain catches you fishing out there you're going to think you caught a shark," I said. "He'll bite your head off. You know how he feels about it."

"He just likes to throw his brass around," Steele said. He walked to the door and flicked his ashes outside, into the sand. Then he put the cigarette to his mouth, inhaled, and turned to face me. After a second or two, he exhaled, thought a moment, then said, "I need to find some bigger bait. You think the locals sell fish in that market down by the seawall?"

"No idea," I said. "I wouldn't worry about it. Maybe you can catch your own bait."

"I need a small tuna or something," he said. "Something big enough to attract a big shark. I'm going to catch one before we move up north. There won't be any fishing up there."

"Bite me!" came a voice from the card game. It was Frankie, the big Italian from New Jersey, who'd played football at Rutgers prior to joining the Marine Corps. He was the only man in the tent with a college degree. People often asked him why he became an enlisted man rather than an officer. He always told them the same thing: he'd joined the Marines because his father, and grandfather, had been Marines. He also said that when his enlistment was up, he was going to go back home and run a car-detailing shop with his brother, and make some real money. His degree was in business, I think.

"How much you take them for this time, Frankie?" Steele said.

"Hundred bucks," Frankie said, raking his winnings into his cover. "You want in?"

Now Steele looked at me. "Come on, Van. Let's win some money."

"You know I don't play cards. I don't have that kind of dough, anyway," I said, which was true. Though we were receiving hazardous-duty pay on top of our regular income, and all of it tax-free for the duration of the war, I was sending most of my paycheck to my bank back home in Oklahoma. Besides, I had little use for money there in Saudi Arabia. About the only things I could buy were bootleg Beatles cassettes, which some of the more enterprising Royal British Marines were hawking from their compound just down the road.

"Here's a perfect opportunity to win some," Steele said. He was sitting on the edge of his cot now, the cigarette smoldering in his fingers. "Come on, dude."

I considered it for a moment. Steele was my best friend, and he certainly knew how to play cards. Whenever money got tight, he'd resort to poker or spades to fill his pocket. He knew all the tricks.

But I couldn't stand the thought of losing my money. Besides, gambling was forbidden. If the company commander walked into the hooch and saw us playing for money, we'd all go up for it. There was also a chance I'd lose a stripe, which meant a reduction in pay.

"Come on, dude!" Steele said, slapping my arm. "Let's win some jack!"

"I don't think so, man."

Just then, the company runner stepped through the door. He was a skinny guy from Virginia, named Pennington, and no one trusted him because he worked for the captain. Everyone got quiet as he removed his sunglasses and glanced around the tent. He'd seen Frankie and the guys playing cards. That much was obvious. But could he tell they were playing for money? If so, he didn't say anything. Frankie was pretty big, so he probably wouldn't mention it even if he had.

Now he looked away from the card game, his eyes leaping from man to man before landing on me. Then, before he could say anything, his eyes drifted away to something just over my right shoulder.

It was Steele's fishing pole. I could see him looking at it, and I almost said something. Because Pennington worked so closely with Captain Garrett, who'd issued the No Swimming/No Fishing order in the first place, I very nearly blurted out that the fishing gear wasn't mine. But he spoke first.

"Van, the captain wants to see you," he said.

I nodded my head. "Be right there."

With that, Pennington turned and left the tent, his hand gripping his rifle sling.

"What'd you do now, Van?" Frankie said from across the hooch, a fan of cards in his hand. "You been gambling again?" The guys around the card game laughed.

I laughed, too. Frankie was funny like that. Then I stood and walked to the door. "Maybe he wants to promote me," I said. "Then I'll come back and whip you guys into shape."

"Later, dude," Steele said as I ducked out of the tent and felt the desert heat attack my face. "Hope you have some ass left when you get back!"

More laughter.

Several minutes later, I stood at attention in front of Captain Garrett, who was seated at his desk.

"At ease, Lance Corporal Van Schuyler," he said.

I relaxed my stance, now standing at parade rest, though my heart was still at attention. Captain Garrett's office had shiny, tile floors and beige-colored walls, on which hung photos of General Colin Powell and President Bush, and on another wall, the U.S. and Marine Corps flags. Prior to the war, this office had belonged to the Saudi harbormaster who supervised operations here at the port. Now, the commercial vessels were gone and in their place were Navy cruisers and battleships, and dozens of inflatable, Zodiac boats, which the Coast Guard used to patrol the harbor.

Captain Garrett was tall and athletic with closely cropped, dark hair that was just beginning to silver above the ears. He had compassionate brown eyes and a gentle demeanor. Most of the guys liked him. Today, however, he looked agitated and irritable. I racked my brain, wondering what I'd done to warrant his attention.

"Lance Corporal Van Schuyler," he said, slowly, as though relishing the anxiety he was causing me. "I understand that you've decided to forego the anthrax vaccination. Is this correct?"

He rested his hard, tattooed arms on the edge of his desk. The shiny silver bars on his collar glinted in the overhead light, while his brown eyes regarded me with a look that shouted disappointment. I had seen that look once before.

During my first year as a fleet Marine, not long after reporting to Camp Pendleton following my graduation from the Marine Corps School of Infantry, I was late getting back to base one Monday after a raucous weekend in Tijuana. As a result, I missed morning formation. That was enough for my boss, Staff Sergeant Wheeler, to write me up for unauthorized absence. On the day of my hearing, I stood in front of Captain Garrett as he announced my punishment—a reduction in rank, loss of a week's pay, and thirty days' extra duty—and then, almost as an afterthought, added that he was suspending this sentence and placing me on probation. Provided I toed the line for the next three months, I could avoid punishment and emerge from all this with only a slight blemish on my record. That's exactly what happened, and I'd been a model Marine ever since . . . until this business with the anthrax vaccinations.

I hated to admit it, but I had to tell the truth. There was no way around it. "Yes sir," I said.

"Lance Corporal Van Schuyler, why have you refused the vaccination? This was a direct order from the battalion commander."

My heart was jumping because I knew I could offer no reason good enough for Captain Garrett. We'd been ordered to receive the anthrax vaccination, and yet I'd refused it even though, technically, my body was property of the U.S. government. It no longer belonged to me. This was hard to fathom, especially for a twenty-year-old.

Not only this, but Captain Garrett didn't play around when it came to enforcing orders. Word was, he was a great guy, and everyone respected him. But you didn't want to get on his bad side. He was a Marine officer, after all, and he expected nothing less than complete loyalty and obedience from his men. I knew there was no excuse good enough for him, so I said the first thing that came to mind.

"Sir, I was afraid of the side effects," I said. Which was true. The Navy doctors had told us the anthrax vaccine we'd been ordered to receive had been tested only on cattle. Which begged the question, at least in my mind: what were the side effects for humans? No one knew, and the Navy corpsmen who administered these vaccines admitted as much. But this didn't matter. We were under orders. We had to take the shot. We didn't have a choice.

What if it caused some disease years later? And how did the government know it wouldn't?

They didn't. But they also told us, in the event we were subjected to anthrax, only those who'd received the vaccination would survive.

I told myself that I had a lot to look forward to in life: getting through the war, leaving the service, starting college. I had my whole life ahead of me. As for the anthrax vaccine, there were just too many unknowns, so I'd refused it.

Captain Garrett did not immediately reply. Except for a ship blowing its whistle out in the harbor, it was silent there in his office. I wondered if he could hear my heart pounding. Then the color of his face seemed to deepen and I could see the blood vessels pulsing in his temples. "The side effects," he said. "What goddamned side effects?"

"Sir..."

"You heard the corpsman in the briefing the other day! There have been no adverse reactions to this drug!"

"Yes, sir."

"Yes, sir, *what?*"

"Yes, sir. There have been no adverse reactions."

I knew the Iraqi army had a history of using biological and chemical weapons against its enemies, and even its own people. And on one hand, it seemed logical that Saddam would use them now, as we were poised to run his troops out of Kuwait and push them back into Iraq. But doing so was also against the Geneva Conventions of War. Saddam knew this. And while he hadn't hesitated to use unconventional weapons against his own people, using them against the coalition forces, and especially the United States, was another matter. He was afraid of us because he knew the U.S. would hold him accountable. I was sure of it. And this was a gamble I was willing to take.

"Then why haven't you had your shot, Lance Corporal Van Schuyler?"

"Sir, I was just concerned about..."

"You're a Marine! You do as you're ordered!" he yelled from his seat. "Is that clear?"

"Yes, sir."

"Good. Now get out of here and get over to BAS and get your shot!"

I snapped to attention. "Yes sir," I said.

"Dismissed."

When I stopped at the battalion aid station, a navy clerk sitting behind a small field typewriter informed me the corpsman who administered the anthrax vaccines was at chow.

"When will he be back?" I asked.

"Probably not until tomorrow morning," the clerk said. "He's going up north this afternoon."

"Is there anyone else around who can give me an anthrax shot?"

"I could," the clerk said. "But I'm not authorized."

"I'll just come back tomorrow," I said, knowing that I'd be on Captain Garrett's radar until I had my shot. Until then, I needed to avoid him.

I left BAS and headed over to the chow hall, where I found Steele making short work of his chicken-and-rice lunch.

He grinned when he saw me. "You got any ass left?" he said, his mouth full.

"Very little."

"What did you do?"

"I didn't do anything," I said as I opened a carton of mango milk. "He thought I'd been fishing in the Gulf. He said he's been getting reports of some Marines fishing down by the seawall. I said it wasn't me."

Steele leaned across the table, his eyebrows raised. I loved messing with him. He always acted like he was immune to the rules and regulations affecting the rest of us, so it was fun seeing him sweat.

"What did you say?"

"I said it wasn't me. I don't even like fishing. Don't have the patience for it."

"Did he mention my name?"

"Well, have you been fishing down there?"

"Why you grinning? Don't fuck around," Steele said. "Does he know it's me?"

"I don't think so," I said. "He just told me to stay out of the water. Said the place is full of sharks."

"He's right," Steele said. "It is. And I want to catch one of them."

"You're not going to catch a shark with that little pole."

"You just watch me," Steele said. "I'll go out after dark, when they can't see me. Just need some bigger bait."

"You're going to be the bait if the captain catches you fishing," I said. "Or the MPs. Don't get caught down there."

"There's nothing to worry about."

"What are you going to do if you catch one?" I said. "I mean, you can't bring a shark back to camp."

"Just let it go," he said. "I fish for sport."

"You don't eat fish?"

"I love fish, but I wouldn't eat a shark," he said. "No one should be eating sharks. Their numbers are in decline from commercial fishing and netting."

"Listen to you," I said. "You sound like a biologist."

"You gotta have sharks," Steele said. "They're at the top of the food chain. Without them, everything's out of balance."

We ate without speaking for several minutes as I listened to the laughing and joking going on around the chow hall. The food was consistently good and every day we had three hot meals. Consequently, the morale among the troops was quite high. Yet, the men were restless. We were tired of sitting around cleaning weapons and standing guard duty and patrolling the harbor. We wanted to go where the action was. We wanted the chance to do what we'd been trained to do. They said we'd be heading north any day now. We were ready.

"I guess you didn't get in on that card game," I said.

Steele shook his head. "We should though."

"Oh, no. You know I don't gamble."

"We can make some jack. I'm great at spades."

"I don't know anything about cards," I said, my mind on the ass chewing Captain Garrett had just handed me, and the fact that I still hadn't received my anthrax vaccine. I hoped the captain wouldn't come into the chow hall now.

"You don't have to," he said, dropping his fork onto his tray and sitting back. "You got me on your team. I can kick anybody's ass in spades. We can win a lot of jack."

"We can also lose it," I said. "Besides, I can't afford to get caught."

"You worry too much, Van. You ought to come shark fishing with me tonight. It's relaxing."

"That's not what I'd call relaxing," I said. "Give me some cold beer and a good-looking redhead."

"Good luck finding that over here."

"Even still, I don't want anything to do with a shark."

The spades game was in full swing when I walked into the hooch after my evening shower. Two others, Jarvis and Purvey, were sitting on their cots, straining to write letters in the dim light. The hooch's doors were open and, outside, men were standing around and leaning on the sandbag walls, laughing and telling stories. The sun was sinking in the west. It looked like a melting orange. After baking all day in the heat, the tent's heavy, canvas walls smelled of petroleum and the desert dust.

"You guys seen Steele?" I said as I approached the men at the card game.

Frankie, the big Italian, shook his head, then slapped his cards onto the table. "Bite me!"

The other card players groaned and shook their heads as Frankie scraped his winnings into his cover. Then, looking up at me, he said, "You and Steele want in?"

"No. We're supposed to stand guard duty in a half hour," I said. "I don't know where he is."

"He's probably fishing again," Jarvis said from across the hooch. "You know how he is."

I glanced at Steele's corner of the tent. His fishing pole was gone. "He'd better not get caught," I said.

Frankie had gathered up the cards and was shuffling them. "Someone said they saw a shark out there today, down by those rocks," he said. "Big ass hammerhead, not twenty feet from shore."

"That's why you won't find me out there swimming," I said.

"Steele keeps saying he's going to catch one before we move up north," Jarvis said. "I'd like to see that."

"Yeah," I said, slinging my rifle over my shoulder. "I guess we'll see."

I left the tent and headed north, past the guard shack at the front gate and away from camp. The seawall was nearly a mile away. According to Steele, this was the best place to fish. Date palms lined either side of the road, and in the waning light I could see a column of Abrams tanks leaving the maintenance compound. Directly ahead, in front of the Royal British Marines' camp, a couple of U.S. Marines were laughing with the British guards. The Brits were great guys, quick with jokes and cigarettes to share, and always wanting to swap gear with us. This was something else we'd been warned against, but that didn't seem to stop the practice.

After a while I spotted a man's silhouette on the opposite side of the road. He was headed in my direction and, when he got close enough, I called out to him. "Thought I was going to have to pull you out of the water."

"I remembered," Steele said. "I was on my way."

I looked at my watch. "You're cutting it close, man. Catch anything?"

He shook his head. "I need a bigger bait for these sharks."

Then the sirens went off.

I turned and sprinted back down the road, past the British compound, and into our camp, running at full speed, hands clamped to my rifle, as the siren wailed. With nightfall coming, it sounded eerie and foreboding. I dove behind a wall of sandbags, and when I sat up, there was Steele, very calmly leaning his fishing pole against the wall.

As I patted the canvas pouch on my hip, ensuring that I had my gas mask should I need it, Steele mumbled something. Then he said, "I left it back at the hooch!"

My heart was thundering, both from the exertion of the run and also from the early-warning sirens. Their wailing was ominous. It was terrifying. Just then, two explosions shook the ground, causing my ears to ring. I could feel the displaced air and I knew this was serious. The U.S. Army hadn't placed a battery of Patriot missiles just down the road for nothing, and the soldiers manning these weapon systems didn't deploy the missiles unless radar picked up a SCUD heading in our direction.

There was commotion all around us as Marines sprinted up and down the corridors between the tents, scrambling to get behind the sandbag walls.

"Shit!" Steele yelled. "I don't have my gas mask!" He started to go over the wall of sandbags. For some reason, I grabbed his shirt and pulled him back down.

"Just stay cool," I said.

The whites of his eyes were showing and his face was dripping with sweat as he looked out over the sandbags. Although we endured these air raids every night, I'd never seen Steele this worried.

I said a quick prayer for both of us. Then I waited, for either the "All clear!" or the command to put on our gas masks.

At times like this, all you could do was sit and hope that the Patriots intercepted the SCUD, or, failing this, that the missile landed somewhere else. The SCUDs were notoriously inaccurate, but they were very effective in inciting terror. You never knew where they'd land.

A moment later, an explosion shook the ground and the sky flashed, as though morning had come crashing in, drunk and disorderly. Suddenly, my face was burning. The hot air smelled like jet wash.

Something was wrong. Men were still running around and shouting, and then another set of Patriots went up like Roman candles in the dark sky, shaking the ground, renewing the ringing in my ears.

Is this it? I wondered. Is this what I get for refusing my anthrax vaccine?

I peeked over the sandbags, wondering where, exactly, the missile had struck, and whether the SCUD had delivered some kind of chemical agent. Was death dispersing into the air around us? The siren continued wailing. To the west, the flames were raging, illuminating the sky as if the sun itself had been shot down.

I tapped Steele on the arm. "Come on," I said, slinging my rifle over my shoulder. "Grab your weapon."

We climbed over the sandbag wall and raced down the main corridor through camp, tents on either side of us. As we neared the fire, the feeling of heat on my face and arms intensified. The smoke irritated my nose and lungs, causing me to cough, my eyes to water.

It was a massive fire and I could feel the heat even from a distance. Marines were running up and down the corridor, carrying buckets of water and stretching hoses. Men were yelling and in the background you could hear the roar of the fire churning, consuming fuel and oxygen, and growing.

To my right, I spotted a group of Marines pushing a water buffalo. I told myself that 400 gallons of water wouldn't make any difference in putting out this fire. It was just too big and intense. But I ran over to help, anyway. Everything was in chaos; people were running with tools and weapons in hand, yelling, cursing. The air-raid siren continued wailing, its cry cracking my ears. Then came the thumping sounds of a low-flying helo. I kept thinking how stupid I'd been for refusing the anthrax shot, while wondering if this was it, if this is what our leaders had been preparing us for.

With the fire burning, engulfing more tents, more oxygen, producing more heat, and growing bigger still, all I could think about was making it through this tragedy, through the night, and into a new day, which seemed so far away.

Then came several small explosions, capped by a sudden burst of gunfire. Everyone hit the deck. I pointed my rifle in the direction of the noise even as I recognized the sounds of the fire consuming an ammunition cache. I pressed myself against the warm ground, trying to stay low and out of the trajectory of stray bullets. We remained like this for several minutes, heads down, cursing our luck and the situation, before someone yelled to get the buffalo down to the fire.

Back on my feet, pushing the cylindrical beast along with a half-dozen others, feeling the heat on its metal fender while my face and hands grew progressively warmer and drier, the water buffalo suddenly stopped rolling. For some reason, I looked back and saw a wall of flames where I'd stood only a few moments before. Steele was nowhere to be seen.

"This way! Down to the water!" someone was shouting.

Marines were speeding by me, on the left and right, yelling at us to get down to the water. I left the water buffalo, certain that it would be engulfed by flames within seconds, then sprinted toward the rocky embankment at the edge of camp. In the distance, lights twinkled from the bridges of docked cargo ships.

Where's Steele? I wondered.

Stumbling over the riprap, I noticed for the first time the wind blowing against my back, agitating the water down below. The air reeked of diesel fuel and smoke. And then my stomach sank.

Grouped there at the edge of the water were hundreds of excited, stunned, and incredulous faces, illuminated in the glow from the fire, which the wind was pushing our way.

And then I saw Steele standing at the edge of the water, rifle slung over his back and gas mask on his hip. He was also holding his fishing rod.

"We're cut off!" he said. "We're fucked."

"They'll send boats to pick us up," I said.

I felt the heat pressing on my face, moving us closer and closer to the water. I smelled the thick, choking smoke from the tents going up in flames. I heard the thumping of the helo above us, and then someone shouting, "Into the water!"

We scrambled down the rocky embankment and into the agitated waters of the Persian Gulf. The fire illuminated the wind-whipped surface in an eerie glow, giving depth and dimension to my fears. I took a step and felt the bottom drop away. Now I treaded water. Behind me, I could hear the fire roaring, closing in on us. I could feel the heat on my head and neck as I paddled away from shore, raking my arms back and forth, kicking my feet to keep my head above the surface. The fire roared as it neared the edge of the sea, consuming everything we'd left behind, its biting heat pushing us farther from the rocks, still farther from shore.

3

Second Chance

A t the bus station I buy a one-way ticket to Biloxi, take a seat in the terminal, build a newspaper wall in front of my face. The information age, technology at the speed of light, mobile telephones, and I'm taking the bus to Biloxi. Going with a few old folks, a fat lady with a hat big enough to shade Montana, and a couple of rowdy kids. Feels like the fifties or something.

After a few minutes I get a tap-tap on my leg. I pull down the paper and there's this little girl, about five, crooked teeth and a T-shirt about three sizes too small.

"Mister, can I have a dollar?" she asks.

"Sorry, Honey. I spent all my dough on this bus," I tell her instinctively, automatically. But looking into her blue eyes, feeling the sharp pangs of guilt rushing through me, I slide my hand into my pocket. I can't help myself. But before I can remove it the woman I take to be her mother comes over, grabs her arm.

"I'm sorry," she says. "She just started doing this about two weeks ago. Taking money from strangers."

"At least she asked," I said with a smile. "There's nothing wrong with that."

When they're gone, I replace the newspaper in front of my face, close enough to smell the ink, my eyes scanning over stories I don't read. I flip a page. Now I spot a little photo in the upper-right corner of page A-3. I feel like I'm looking into a mirror. I read the part about being released on Thursday, the serial burglar who broke into the district attorney's house. They dedicate two tiny paragraphs to my release, describing the case, the prison sentence, and the child neglect and string of burglaries that sent me there. Strange, but they don't mention the fact that I'm on parole for the next year, which means I have to walk a fine line or else I go back to the joint.

Yeah, yeah, I know all that, I tell myself. Burglary. So what? I've let all that go. It's not the burglaries that bother me. It's the memory of leaving my son, Adam, in the car that night while I went out to pull that job. It's the guilt I felt when I got caught, when they cuffed me, knowing Adam was going to wake up to the police instead of his father. I served my time and paid for the burglaries, but I can't shake the guilt from leaving my son alone that night. I'm reminded of this every time I see a child and it makes me wonder how Adam is these days, what he's doing, if he's playing sports or planning to go to college some day. He should be starting high school this fall.

The bus pulls in 15 minutes late and passengers crowd the steps, getting off, getting on. The air inside the bus is heavy with the scent of people—sweat, perfume, cigarette smoke. I take a seat near the back, over the wheels. The seats around me are empty when I sit down, but moments later an elderly lady appears, skinny red-headed boy hanging from her hand like an ugly purse. She looks around like a hen searching for a nest, turning her head this way and that, then decides on the seats directly across the aisle from mine. The boy looks over at me from behind a cloud of freckles, smiles, smacks his gum. I wonder where his father is.

The old lady glances at me a couple of times, then picks up a newspaper and busies herself. A while later I hear the paper drop. I can feel her studying my profile, but I don't look at her. Quickly she takes the boy by the hand and scurries off toward the front of the bus.

It's a little over 200 miles to Biloxi so I lean back in the seat, close my eyes and listen to the diesel engine grumbling, feeling every bump in the road. When we arrive, I leave the bus station and head over to the hardware store, spend my last seven dollars on a garden spade. It's a small one; fits inside my back pocket. Then I walk three blocks south, west a block, and another two south. Just ahead is the Gulf of Mexico. I'm walking through a neighborhood of giant antebellum homes situated on huge lots. The yards are full of these tall pine trees you see all over the South, smelling clean and green, and mixing with the salty ocean air to remind me I'm not in prison anymore. There are also live oaks with Spanish moss hanging from the branches. The grass is so green it looks artificial. I want to drop down in it, roll around, feel the soft blades on my neck. But I have a job to do, so I keep walking.

The house is just up ahead. I could recognize it in my sleep. Jeep in the driveway. A small woodlot insulates it from the neighbor's place. But there are people sitting on the front porch. This is a job that'll have to wait until dark.

I go down to the beach, take off my shoes, slosh through the water. The waves are sweeping the floor of the sea, pushing the debris and whitewash up onto the beach, then retreating. A moment later the waves roar in with another load of marl and sea-weed. I notice a couple of ships way out on the horizon. Probably cargo ships. They don't seem to be moving. But when I look at them again a minute or so later, they've changed positions. Gulls and terns scream from the air, searching, hovering, diving into the sea, emerging with tiny fish that glint like newly minted coins. The wind is blowing, the sun is shining, and the roar of the surf is invigorating. Life is all around me, which is so refreshing after spending five years in a tiny steel-and-concrete cell. I wish I had a fishing rod and a few lures. I'd like to try my luck.

After a while I break out the spade, build a sand castle near the water's edge. Then I move up onto the dry sand and stretch out, place my cap over my face and close my eyes. When I open them again it's nearly dark.

The cicada chorus in the trees is in full swing when I take off down the beach. It's night now and I feel safe. I locate the house and move into the yard, kneel beneath a massive cypress tree. The windows are illuminated like a country clubhouse, one side of the deck hugging the back door, the other side cascading into the yard. I study the windows, then the deck, then the trees nearest the house.

It was the biggest tree, I tell myself. Huge. I move farther into the yard, kneel, listen. A light breeze wafts voices my way from a house down the beach. I smell cigar smoke, hear laughter, feel the hunger pains in my stomach, see nothing but trees and a few giant homes, sense that I may be screwing up. I'm sweating profusely. Fourteen hours out of the pen and I'm risking going right back, for what? A little bit of cash? The promise of a new life?

I creep closer to the house, deeper into private property, feeling pine needles crunch beneath my feet, smelling the richness of the trees. Roosting birds cackle and clatter up in the branches. It's a clear night and through holes in the canopy I can see stars. I hear the surf growing distant behind me as I move deeper into the yard.

Maybe the other trees have grown. Maybe they're all the same size now. Then I see what I think is the tree. It's as big as the others, branch like an elbow coming off one side of the trunk. It's unmistakable. Of course it's the one.

I move up to the giant pine, put my back against the trunk and count ten paces out, directly toward the beach, as though the tree and I are in a duel. Then I pull out the spade and start digging.

When I get about a foot down into the soil I hear voices coming from the house. A man comes out onto the deck, cigarette glowing in his right hand. He takes a seat. It's him, all right. The DA man. Though I'm far enough away that I can't make out his facial features, I can still see him in my mind: him in that courtroom, in the newspapers, that smirk on his face after I was convicted. He is physically unremarkable—average height, build, features—but he's the DA man, so people listen to what he says, especially judges. I wonder what he would say if he knew some of his missing money was buried in his own backyard.

I'm not worried about him seeing me because the floodlights illuminate only the open yard. I'm well inside the trees, in the dark. But then I hear voices behind me. I hit the dirt.

Turns out it's only a couple walking on the beach. A minute later they're gone, but the DA man is still on the deck. I keep my eyes on him, watching the cigarette cherry rise and fall, adjusting my grip on the spade. I can smell the cigarette smoke. After several minutes, he stands, drops the cigarette butt into a can and goes back inside the house. I resume digging.

Eventually I hit something solid, dig some more and pull out the Mason jar. I twist the lid off, dump the contents into my hand. They consist of two keys and a roll of money, thirteen hundred and change, as I recall. I'll have to count it later. I dump the jar back into the hole, along with the spade, push the dirt back in, cover everything with leaves and pine needles. Then I retreat back to the beach, disappear into the night, stopping once to wash my hands in the surf.

After breakfast the next morning, I walk over to the storage unit owned by a distant uncle, where several years ago I stored a car. The car's pretty dusty, cobwebs connecting antennae to mirrors. I open the hood, look the engine over, check the spark-plug connections. To my surprise she fires right up. It's a '78 Monte Carlo, dated, dusty, hasn't seen the light of day in five years. But I've got wheels now, so I drive.

West. And then north. I don't know exactly where I'm going, so I'm in no particular hurry to get there. I just want to get out of Mississippi, away from the papers, the prodding eyeballs, the people who come up asking for money. You might say I'd planned for this day, planned for my post-prison life by stashing away some dough. I figured the last place anybody would look for it was the DA man's backyard. It's not much, but I hope it's enough to give me a head start on a new life.

I'm supposed to check in with my parole officer once a week and report on my job prospects, let him know what I'm doing. And I'm not supposed to leave the state of Mississippi. But that's exactly what I'm going to do. I have to put my past behind me. So I think I'm just going to drive on and hope that I can find something quiet and low-key, where folks won't notice me. I need to go somewhere else and become a new person.

I was supposed to do eight years, but got out early because I made no trouble, did what I was told, and because the state's going bankrupt housing and feeding petty joint smokers and kids with no direction in life. Truthfully, some of those kids reminded me of myself at their age—running around unsupervised, hanging around the wrong crowds, getting into trouble. Looking back, if my parents hadn't divorced, if I hadn't spent my summers unsupervised and running with Lenny—the older kid who lived down the street, who taught me how to break into houses—I like to think I'd have turned out differently. That's all behind me. There's nothing I can do about it now but change. I want to become the man I wish I could have been, that I should've been. Whatever that is.

I stop for the night in a small town just outside Fort Smith, Arkansas, walk into an all-night diner and order fried chicken, mashed potatoes. There's a newspaper on the table. I flip to the classifieds.

The ad says:

FARM MANAGER NEEDED
LARGE SWINE OPERATION IN
EASTERN OKLAHOMA.
GOOD PAY AND HOUSING FOR RIGHT PERSON.

I call and inquire. Next morning I go out and meet the guy.

"Bo Cartwright," I say, extending my hand.

"Cartwright? Any kin to Ben Cartwright?" says the man, laughing. He's a tall, lanky guy with cowboy boots, salt-and-pepper hair. I guess that he's twenty years older than me, probably in his mid-fifties. With his boots, hat, big belt buckle, he looks like he ought to be running a quarter horse operation somewhere. Says his name is Sam Roberts. "Know anything about hog farming?"

"I was raised on a farm," I tell him, recalling the twenty acres in south Mississippi where I had once lived with my parents before they split up. Sam's place is much more modern than any farm I've seen and it's obviously well-maintained. We're standing on the edge of a large circle driveway, covered in gravel, surrounded by beige metal barns on three sides. The barns appear new and the grounds around them very clean. I don't see a bit of litter and the grassy strips separating the buildings are neatly trimmed. Each barn has a vent fan spinning up in the loft, just beneath the roof peak, and the air smells of swine and dirt, grain. "We had a lot of hogs and cattle."

"Where you from?" he asks.

Too many questions, I think. What does it matter? "Texas. Been working as an underwater welder on some of the cargo ships down there."

"Now that's an interesting occupation," says the man. "What makes you want to leave something like that?"

"Way too dangerous for me. There was an explosion a couple of months ago, killed two of the guys. I figured I'd get out while I could."

"Get while the getting's good, huh? Well, why don't we take a walk through some of the barns? I'll show you around the place."

Sam says that he likes the fact that I know how to weld, tells me that a good welder always has a place on the farm. Then he asks me if I'm married; I tell him no. Divorced. When he asks me if I have any kids, I tell him I have a son, but that I don't see him. It turns out that Sam is single, a widower. Wife died of cancer seven years back. He's got a son who's eleven, a couple of hands around the place that I'd have to keep in line. Tells me they're good workers, but they need leadership. Maybe I do too.

Inside the first barn it's warm and the smell of hogs and sawdust permeates the air. The floors are impeccably clean and we move down a slatted walkway, pens on either side. In each pen there is a white sow with piglets. Looks to be four dozen pens.

"This here's the farrowing barn," he says. "This is a farrow-to-finish operation. We raise them from the time they're born, keep them up to about two hundred and twenty pounds, then we get them out of here."

"That's a lot of pork."

"Well, we run about two hundred head a month to market."

We stop at a corner pen, look at the little white products rooting around in the sawdust. A metal self-feeder runs along one side of the pen, surrounded by a red cage.

"Creep feeder," Sam says. "Had to install these in every pen. We were losing too many babies. Say, you know the gestation for hogs?"

"Something like three months, I think."

He lights a Camel.

"Three months, three weeks, three days, and sometimes three hours," he says. "They're pretty predictable."

"Why you raise Yorks?" I ask.

"The mother breed," he tells me. "We average about fifteen babies a litter. We used to run Durocs, but you only get about eight with them."

We walk to the far end of the barn, where a couple of Mexicans are bottle feeding runts. Sam introduces me and I say hello. The piglets are as cute as puppies. I can't get over how tiny they are, but in six months' time they'll be heavier than the men now holding them.

"You always take on the runts like that?"

"We don't get many runts," Sam says. "When we do, we get them started and give them to the 4-H kids."

We leave the farrowing barn, move into a larger building. Vent fans hum in the loft. The stench of hogs stronger here. Fluorescent lights in the ceiling shine down on the concrete walkways and pens full of adult hogs. "This is the finishing barn," he says. "We put them in here at about one-forty, finish them off and get them out."

Sam's takes a call on his cell phone and after a "yeah, yeah, all righty then," he slides it into his back pocket.

"Well, Bo, what do you think?"

"Looks like you've got a first-class operation here. I'll do my best to make you a good hand."

"Job's yours if you want it. You can start tomorrow. Pay is ten an hour to start, and after six months we'll look at putting you on salary."

"Sounds good to me."

"That includes the little house out back. That'd be all yours."

"I appreciate it, Sam," I say, shaking his hand.

"Now we don't allow no drinking, no dope, anything like that."

"I'm clean," I say. He looks down at my jeans, tennis shoes.

"You'd better get yourself some boots and gloves. They've got them up at the hardware store."

"I'll do it. See you in the morning."

"One more thing," he says. He places his hands on his hips, looks me in the eye. "I'll need to get some references from you, if you have any."

My heart jumps up in my throat, mouth goes dry. I was afraid of this. The production factory upstairs is churning, but the output is nil. I say the first thing that comes to mind.

"Well, the guy I was working for in Texas is one of them went down in that explosion. I can give you the number, maybe someone else can talk to you."

"That'll be fine."

That afternoon I pull into a drive-in and order a steak sandwich and onion rings, which I eat in my car. I feel safe here in the car, safe from curious eyes, unexpected questions. Though I've done my time, I can't shake this feeling of paranoia. Whenever I interact with another person, I catch myself wondering what they're thinking, whether they suspect that I'm an ex-convict. It's hard to look people in the eye. Somehow I managed to do it with Sam. Does he suspect that I've just got out of the pen? Does he think I'm lying about my background? Should I just shove off to another town, another job where the boss doesn't ask so many questions?

As for my references, I have none, at least none that I could give for a job. Sam's bound to find out. But my intentions are honorable and I know I can make him a good hand. So I decide to go to the hardware store and buy boots, gloves, jeans and a pair of wire cutters. But if Sam checks my references I'm screwed. Won't need any of it. I make it a point to keep the receipt.

Next morning I show up at the barns bright and early. The Mexicans are already there and I introduce myself again, tell them I'm the new manager. One goes by Tug, the other tells me his name is Hector. They both seem to know what they're doing because they're always busy and don't ask many questions.

A little while later Sam appears, gives me the new-employee orientation, hands me keys to the trucks, tractors, shows me where the tools are kept. He also shows me where the medicine cabinet is because you're always needing bandages and antibiotic ointments on the farm. I notice a Folgers coffee can inside the cabinet, faded and scratched from age, with a thin hole in the lid.

Sam gives me his cell-phone number and tells me to give him a call if I need anything or if I have any questions. I fully expect him to hit me up about the number I'd given him for the reference, but he doesn't mention it. Then he tells me he's got business in town, drives off in his pickup.

Later, I get Tug and Hector to help me out clipping needle teeth. Hector distracts the three-hundred pound sow while Tug grabs a squealing piglet, holds it while I clip the teeth. We move away from the infuriated sow while we do this. She expresses her anger by head-butting the steel panel, squealing, biting the bars. When we finish with one we return the pig to its mother while Hector distracts and Tug snatches another. We go from one pen to the next. It takes nearly six hours to get through them all. On the last litter, the sow rams the fence panel where Hector is perched, knocking him to the floor. Luckily, he falls onto the walkway, outside the pen.

A little later, a young boy enters the barn, baseball cap turned backward on his head. He walks up, tells me his name's Jeff, to let him know if I need anything.

"I know where my old man keeps the keys to the diesel, petty cash and all that," he says. "You need anything just let me know. You need some help right now?" he asks.

"We're just flushing the pens. I appreciate it, though," I say. Jeff's work ethic surprises me. Why would a kid want to work out here if he didn't have to? Then I notice the scar on his arm. It's pink and smooth, runs from wrist to elbow. I guess it's an old wound, but it's healed well. I know a little bit about scars, wounds. Saw a lot of them in the pen.

"If you need anything just let me know," he says. "I'm going to run this place some day."

"Thanks for the offer, buddy."

Tug must have caught me noticing Jeff's scar because after the boy leaves he tells me how it happened. Turns out, Jeff got his arm caught in one of the fence panels over in the boar pen. "Ripped it open quick," he says.

I go back to flushing the pens and when I reach the end of the aisle, I look up and notice the medicine cabinet on the wall. Seeing it, I'm reminded of the coffee can inside, so I go over and check it out. I peel off the plastic lid to find the can full of money. My heart kicks up the pace a beat or two. There must be $500 in here, anyway. I replace the lid, return the can to the cabinet and get back to hosing down the pens. That's a lot of money to be sitting in a coffee can out in the barn.

One morning shortly after I hire on Sam comes into the barn, asks how I'm getting along. Each time I see the man I expect him to bring up the reference. But he never does, which tells me he either called, got a wrong number and doesn't care, or he hasn't called at all. I figure the odds aren't in my favor, and every time I think about this it bothers me more because I'm starting to like this place. We're out here in the country, just Sam and Jeff and me, and Hector and Tug. Nobody asks questions. Nobody messes with us.

I mention Jeff coming out to introduce himself.

"I don't mind him coming out here," says Sam. He jams a cigarette between his lips, lights up. He's wearing a straw cowboy hat this morning, faded Wranglers with razor-blade creases burned white. "But he's not to lend a hand in any way. I don't want him messing around out here and getting hisself hurt again. You heard what happened with the boar?"

I nod. "The guys told me."

"Well, I worry about his safety out here. These hogs are big and strong, and they can do a lot of damage if you're not paying attention. And when they have a litter, look out. Momma hogs are the worst. But you know all that," he says, waving a smoke trail with his hand.

"I'll keep him out of trouble," I say.

"Well, since his momma's been gone, I have to really look after him. I mean, he's big enough to look after hisself, but I've kinda gotta be his momma too. You know." He takes a long drag, exhales, observes the hogs. "I want that boy to go to college some day. Want him to have something more than this," he says. "It'd be too easy for him to fall into this and never know anything else."

My mind races back two decades and I remember Lenny showing me how to slide that library card into the back door of that house, sliding it in and pushing, the lock falling and the door swinging open. No signs of forced entry, he'd said. They probably won't even know they've been hit for a few days. That's how you cover your tracks. And he was right. For a long time this worked. It worked so well I fell into that rut and never found anything else.

"I'll keep an eye out for him, Sam," I say, partly to settle his nerves, partly to get him to clear out so that I can get back to work. After another cigarette, he leaves.

"You can turn it up a little now," I yell to Hector. He looks over and I give him the thumbs up. Then he walks to the little transistor radio hanging from baling wire on the barn wall, turns up the volume and sounds of accordions, guitars and mariachis fill the air. It's happy music and even though I can't understand the lyrics, I like it. Each day I'm able to put my past a little farther behind me, and this makes me feel like I'm moving on with my life. I thought the other day about calling my probation officer, but he'd probably throw a fit that I'm living out of state. Besides, I'm working now, leading an honorable life, staying out of trouble. Just keep my nose clean for the next year and I'm home free, I tell myself.

As the days and weeks roll by, the thought of the reference check goes from a sharp, nagging pain in my side to something like a name I can't remember. Each week I figure that Sam will walk up to me, tell me I gave him the wrong number, ask for another. But he doesn't. I attribute this, in part, to the job I'm doing. For the first time maybe in my whole life I feel I'm living up to my potential. Not that this is all I could ever do, but that Sam can trust me to look after his enterprise, his livelihood. That means a lot to me, and I try to do the best job I can. There haven't been any accidents with the crew. We haven't lost any hogs. Hector and Tug seem to be getting along all right. They work hard and the farm is running smoothly. Every Friday I take a trailer of finished hogs to market, bring back the ticket, deposit a hundred dollars in the coffee can and close up shop for the night. We're up to $733 in petty cash right now. With the balance growing every week, I've taken it upon myself to check the can twice every day just to make sure none of the bills grow legs and walk off. It's all there. Watching it add up so quickly has inspired me to begin saving some of my earnings.

Each week I put back half my paycheck, buy a money order with the other half and mail it to my son in Texas. I got his mother's address off the Internet. The first time I mailed him some money I included a note saying I was sorry for what I'd done, that I knew this wouldn't make up for it, but I hoped it would help somehow. Even though I don't hear from him, I feel like it's the right thing to do. Maybe some day he'll forgive me.

At night I sit around the little house they've given me. Not much to do, so I take a shower, pop a frozen dinner in the microwave, eat and read. I do a lot of reading. On those occasions when I go into town for dinner, I pull into a drive-in and eat in my car. Don't much care to sit in a café by myself. I'm too paranoid. Prison does that to you. It follows you like a storm cloud. But things are slowly getting better, and the more I think about it, the harder I work. This helps.

One evening I'm sitting around the house, reading, and there's a knock at the door. It's Jeff. He walks in wearing shorts, a baggy T-shirt and a pair of old boots, looks like he's just in from safari.

"What's going on?"

"I came to see if you wanted to go fishing down at the creek," he says. "My friend Robbie was supposed to go but his old man made him cut the grass."

"Sure," I say. "What do you fish for?"

"Catfish, mostly. There's some bass down there, but mostly catfish."

"You have a fishing pole I could use?"

"Oh, you won't need a pole. We're noodling," he says.

"Noodling?"

"Yeah, with your hands," he says. He grins, adjusts his cap. Jeff is brimming with confidence. It's hard to believe he's only eleven. "You ever done it?"

"No, I've always used a pole to catch my fish."

"It's a blast," he says. "All you need's a pair of gloves. Robbie doesn't even use them."

"Well let me get my gloves, then. I'm not that tough."

We walk down the hill to the creek, skirting the edge of a corn-field, stalks like green minutemen standing in formation. Jeff carries a rope and a pair of gloves. He grows more and more excited the closer we get to the creek. The air is heavy with humidity. Grasshoppers fly out in front of our feet like rocks we've kicked.

When we reach the creek we walk the sandy bank down-stream to a small bridge. There are six concrete pillars supporting the bridge. The middle two are situated smack in the middle of the creek, surrounded by water.

Pointing to these pillars, Jeff says, "It's a little deeper out there. Should be some fish."

"How deep?" I ask, remembering Sam's concern about Jeff's safety. For a moment I consider saying something, wondering whether I should stop him. But then the realization hits me that Jeff isn't unsupervised. I'm here with him. He's safe.

"It shouldn't be more than shoulder-deep for you."

"How do you grab the fish?"

"I go under and do it," he says. "Unless you want to go first."

"No, I guess I'll just watch this one. You swim okay, I guess."

"Me? I'm a good swimmer."

"What does your dad say about you doing this?"

"He doesn't say anything, but he doesn't always know. I mean, he wouldn't care. He knows I know what I'm doing."

We move into the water. Jeff puts on the gloves and wraps one end of the rope around his right hand, like a bull rider fighting the butterflies in his stomach before the big moment. He puts the other end between his teeth.

"Okay, quiet now," he says. "Move real easy."

We close in on the pillars, water rings radiating out from our knees, then our waists, as we sink into deeper water. About five feet away from the structures the sandy creek bottom falls off. I move to the edge, feeling with my feet, watching Jeff's torso shrink into shoulders, then a head. On his face is a look of stern concentration. With only his head visible on the surface, the rope in his mouth, he reminds me of a retriever.

"They're here," he says, spitting out the rope.

"How do you know?"

"I can feel them with my feet. Feels like there's a big one down there, too."

"What now?"

"I'm going under. When I find one I'll slip this rope through its gill."

"They let you do that?"

"These are momma catfish," he says. "Flatheads. They're on the nest right now, in these logs. They'll bite you when get your hands down there. That's how they protect their nests."

The butterflies hatch in my stomach and I'm only watching. I feel like I should do something to help, but there doesn't seem to be anything to do but watch. I watch closely.

Jeff takes a big breath, grabs the loose rope and disappears into the murky water. I feel the bottom sloping off toward the pillar. It must be five or six feet deep, I think.

After a few seconds Jeff shoots up out of the water, chest heaving, mouth open wide. He wipes his eyes.

"What happened?"

"There's a good one down there, but it closed its mouth when I tried to put the rope through," he says, heaving. He holds up his glove. "Bit down on my hand."

"What now?" I ask.

He holds up a hand, inhales deeply, disappears again. Seconds later he appears, spitting carbon dioxide, sucking oxygen.

"They moved off."

"You want to try that other pillar?"

He looks, shakes his head, moves toward the bank.

"Let's try a different place. There's a logjam just downstream. It usually has a good fish or two."

A few minutes later we come to a bend in the creek. A lazy current pushes around the far side, slowly carving away the clay bank. The water on the inside of the bend is shallow. The sandy bottom slopes away into deeper water on the far side. On one end of the bend is a pile of logs, driftwood and brush. Residue from past floods. We approach the pile from the shallow side.

"All right," Jeff says. "We'll find a good log and I'll need you to plug up one end while I reach in and grab the fish."

"You're going to reach your hand into the log?"

"Yeah. I do it all the time," he says. "We might find a big fish here. This is where the females come to lay their eggs, in these logs."

Jeff winds the rope around his right hand, bites the other with his teeth. As we approach the logs, the smell of dead fish permeates the air. Jeff works his way around the logs, head just above water, feeling with his hands, reaching into the debris pile.

"Okay, found one," he says.

"Is it a big one?"

"A log, not a fish. It's good and hollow, though. It should have one inside."

"Tell me what to do," I say, moving in close.

"Got your gloves on?"

"Yeah."

"Stuff them into the other end of the log right over here," he says. "That way the fish can't escape."

We're all but inside the log pile, muddy water flowing around us. My hands are shaking. Should I say something to Jeff? Should I stop him from noodling? I keep telling myself he knows what he's doing. And he seems to.

He takes the rope from his mouth, reaches into the log. It's only inside for a second.

"Ouch!" he shouts. He jerks his arm from the hole as if he's been burned. "Shit!"

"What happened?" I ask, yanking my hands free of the log. About that time a long black shape appears just beneath the surface, slicing back into the logs where it disappears, causing my stomach to boil.

"Snake!" he says, holding his hand up, clenching his wrist. He stumbles out of the water.

"Let me see." Just above his wrist are two fang marks the size of pinheads, blood oozing out. I pull out my pocketknife. "This is going to hurt." I make two slits across the fang marks, hold his wrist up to my mouth.

Not long after I went to prison a couple of inmates tried to escape by threatening one of the guards with a copperhead snake. As it turned out, the snake bit the inmate who was handling it and I watched as one of the guards used his knife to score the fang marks and then suck out the venom. It worked and the inmate survived, though I never understood why the guard made any attempt to help the convict after what he'd done.

"Clamp down on your arm right here," I tell him. Again I suck blood, feeling the warmth against my tongue, then spit it out. "Come on, Jeff. We've got to get you to the doctor. I couldn't tell. Was it a cottonmouth?"

He nods, holding his arm. "I think so."

I grab his other arm and we climb the bank, walk back to the farm. Jeff wants to run.

"Take it easy, buddy," I tell him. "Just calm down and you'll be all right."

"Damn, it hurts," he says, jaw clenched, sweat beading on his forehead.

We reach the farm and climb into one of the trucks. I don't see Sam's truck, so I punch the gas and we take off for town. On the way, I look over and notice his wrist is swelling. Jeff leans out the window, vomits.

"Snake bite," I tell the lady in the ER. "I think it was a cotton-mouth." She gives me a clipboard with some papers to fill out. A nurse takes Jeff and they disappear down the hallway. "His dad will fill these out when he gets here. You got a phone I can use?"

I hesitate to call, only because I know Sam's going to blow his top. It's going to cost me my job, I'm sure. But Sam needs to know that his son is hurt.

He arrives thirty minutes later, walks directly to Jeff. He doesn't look at me.

"How are you, Sport?" he asks. "You got to hang in there. I know it hurts, but you'll be all right."

"Was it a moccasin?"

"I think so," I tell him. I feel ridiculous. He hired me to look after his operation and I can't even keep his son out of trouble. And looking at Jeff, I'm reminded that this isn't the first time I've let a child down. Any minute I expect he'll tell me to hit the road. I don't know where I'll go or what I'll do. I guess I'll be back in the car, driving until I stumble into something else. Things have been going so well. Too well, I guess.

Sam shakes his head. "How long ago did he get bit?"

"About forty minutes."

He shakes a Camel out of the crinkling pack in his hands, jams it between his lips.

"Sir, you can't smoke in here," the nurse says.

"Oh, sorry." He removes the cigarette, mumbles something, takes a seat. "I'll stay with him now. You can go ahead and go."

Sam is uneasy, fidgety. I wonder if he's that addicted to nicotine. Jeff is lying on the bed, shivering, his face pale and distant. I feel horrible and now I can't stop thinking about Adam.

"Hang in there, buddy," I tell him. "You'll be all right."

I leave the ER, follow the signs through the hospital to the cafeteria. There I buy a cup of coffee and walk to a waiting area I'd passed on the way. It's my fault he's in here, I tell myself. My fault. I didn't stop him from getting into the creek. I didn't look after him like Sam asked me to. For a few minutes, I consider walking back to the ER and resigning. But I decide to stick it out and see what happens. I was never one for confrontation, anyway.

The following Friday I'm spraying down the finishing barn, the water hose in my hands reminding me of the snake that I can't seem to get out of my mind. The doctor fixed Jeff up and he's walking around now like nothing happened. Kids are resilient like that.

Sam comes in to give me my check as usual. He lights a Camel and says, "Say, did I ever tell you I served in the army, in Vietnam?"

"I don't think so."

"You remind me of this old boy I served with. Name was Ramsey. He was from California. He was my squad leader and boy he was just shit-hot. Knew everything about everything. Taught us all we needed to know. Looked after us younger guys like a father. He went on leave one time and didn't come back for a while. When he returned, why, the colonel was ready to bust him down to private. The platoon sergeant stood up for him, though. Said Ramsey was his best soldier. Asked the colonel to spare him. He never lost a stripe."

I smile and shake my head, wondering why Sam is telling me this story.

"It wasn't just because of his technical knowledge. It was his sincerity that saved him. He loved being a soldier and he gave his heart to his job. When your heart's in the right place, you can overlook a lot. I can tell you enjoy working out here and I sure appreciate what you did for Jeff. He might not have made it if you hadn't been here to get him to the doc."

"Well, I didn't do much. But I'm glad he's all right."

"Thanks again, Bo," he says as he walks out of the barn.

After he leaves I open the envelope to find an extra week's pay. Note inside says he appreciates what I did, thanks me for looking after Jeff.

A couple of weeks after the snakebite incident, I ask Sam for the following Monday off, tell him I want to head down to the Gulf and do some fishing. "Redfish," I say. "Tomorrow's the full moon and they'll get a big tide for the next couple of days. Fishing should be great this weekend."

"Bring us back some fresh fish to eat," he says.

Before leaving, I go back into my room and remove $1,347 from one of the jars where I keep my money, stuff it into a large, padded envelope, seal it shut. I can't remember the address, but I don't need it anyway. I'm going to make an in-person delivery that I hope will help clear my conscience.

The envelope stays on the front passenger seat the entire day, all the way down to the coast. I arrive in Biloxi and drive immediately to the neighborhood, to the big house surrounded by pines and cypress and live oaks. I park in the street, in front of the house, and pick up the envelope.

I debate whether I should leave it on the porch, or ring the doorbell. I glance around, across the street, check my rearview mirror, wondering if I'm being watched. Just do it, I tell myself. Get it over with and you'll feel better.

A few minutes later I'm still in the car debating what to do when I hear another vehicle approaching behind me. Glancing into the rearview mirror, I spot a police cruiser, which, to my surprise, pulls in behind me, lights flashing. Oh, no!

My heart races. My stomach has that light, jittery feeling I used to get before I would break into a house. I haven't felt it in a while now, but it's unmistakable. Through the mirror, I watch the officer get out of the car and approach me.

"Afternoon, sir. Can you please state your business here?"

What can I say? I look down at the envelope in my hand, hold it up to show the officer. "I was just going to make a delivery."

At this, the officer steps back from the car door, places his right hand on his sidearm. Then he draws the weapon out of the holster, points it at me. "Sir, please step out of the car, slowly, and place the envelope on the ground."

I can't believe what's happening. Why me? Why now?

Perhaps it's being in such close proximity to law enforcement—the policeman, the district attorney's house—but I am suddenly very aware of my parole officer. I haven't thought about him in months. I thought I could just keep my nose clean for a year and then fade into obscurity, but now that seems like such a stupid idea.

I'm still face down on the ground, hands cuffed behind my back, when I notice a second police cruiser speeding toward us. But instead of thinking about going back to prison, all I can think about is how I've let Sam down and how he's going to wonder what happened to me when I don't show up for work next Monday. He's going to think I flaked out on him. Even though I got Jeff to the doctor when he needed help, even though the money in the coffee can is all there, I'm still going to let him down. And that's what bothers me most.

4

Under the Bar

I've eaten only half of my double-steak, triple-bacon Megaburg-er with cheese when the drive-through chime buzzes behind the counter, jolting the cluster of Burger Barn employees into mo-tion, thinning them, and shocking me into a state of urgency, re-minding me that time is running out. I've got an appointment.

I take one last bite of the burger and stuff a sweet-potato wedge into my mouth, then push myself up from the table, which tips under my hands. The workers behind the counter turn and watch. One places a hand over his mouth.

Go ahead, I want to say. Get a good look. It's not the first time and it won't be the last.

It hurts. But I get it. It must be quite a thing to see someone my size pry himself from one of these tiny tables. If it were for anything less than the Megaburger; if work wasn't so stressful, so demanding, so wholly consuming; if not for the need to detach myself from the world long enough to catch my breath, I wouldn't subject myself to all this.

On the way out the door I pass a young woman squirting ketchup onto her tray. *Pump, squirt. Pump, squirt.* There's a little boy with her, stretching, straining, trying to reach a French fry.

I'd like to have a talk with his mother. I have lots I could tell her, but it's not my place. *Pump, squirt. Pump, squirt.*

Now I'm aware of my own pumping heart, the blood squirting through my veins—functions no doubt impeded by my fast-food diet, which my doctor says is killing me.

I know he's right. But eating the way he wants me to just isn't realistic. Not for me.

By the time I reach my car, I'm out of breath. Slowly, I lower myself into the driver's seat, letting go at the last second and falling into place behind the steering wheel. I rest for a moment before fastening the seatbelt. It's 10:51 a.m., nine minutes until my appointment. No way I'm going to make it on time. I feel my heart pumping and pounding, expanding and collapsing, the blood bursting through my temples. I turn the air conditioner on high and pitch my phone onto the passenger seat beside some napkins and an empty bag from the last drive-through I visited. Then I grab the seatbelt and pull. It seems I'm pulling for a long time, but eventually I have enough belt for this big body. Finally, I click the buckle into place and, still short of breath, drive out of the parking lot, the clock in my head flashing:

11:00 . . . 11:00 . . . 11:00

Then the numbers blank out, replaced by a series of hash-marks:

I should have left earlier. I shouldn't have left work at all. I should have eaten a grilled-salmon salad. I should take better care of myself!

These regrets. They're built up like a physical barrier, blocking my way to a more fulfilling life. Sometimes I tell myself it's not too late, but then I look up at the clock and realize I've put in another twelve-hour shift and will have to do the very same thing again the next day, and the next, just to keep up. Who has time to be healthy?

I look again at my phone. Six minutes till eleven.

Then it buzzes. Another message from work. This one from Doug, my new boss.

With sixty-seven unread e-mails and a supervisor spoiling to exert his authority, my instincts tell me to open the message, to let Doug know I'm connected, that I'm still working, even when I'm not. I know I shouldn't e-mail while driving, but that's exactly what I'm doing when I glance up and notice red taillights flashing, warning me to back off the gas and relax. I hit the brakes and drop the phone, telling myself to forget about it until I get to the doctor's office.

A moment later, the phone buzzes again. Sixty-eight messages.

Work, e-mails, the traffic: they converge with one another right here in my car, in my head, in my heart, edging me toward the panic threshold, undermining the reason I stopped at the burger joint in the first place, which was to relax. Eating always calms me. Food is about the only thing, besides my dog, Max, that doesn't judge me, doesn't try to guilt me for my girth. Wish I could say the same for my company.

I'm a recruiter. I find jobs for people. And since being passed over for supervisor last month, I've tried analyzing everything about myself in an effort to understand why Chuck Stafford, my boss and president of the company, would choose to promote someone less experienced and knowledgeable, and with fewer industry connections. But I already know the answer. Doug Rankin is 10 years younger. He's also much, much thinner.

Sometimes I ask myself why I care. As a supervisor, I'd be subjected to more meetings, stress, and irregularity in my schedule. For a creature of habit, like myself, that's not particularly appealing.

But a promotion would also engender more respect from those around me, those who view my obesity as an obscenity. I can see it in their eyes. When my boss told me he was promoting Doug because "it's in the best interest of the company," what he was really saying is that appearances matter. More than experience. More than determination. Even more than desire. Deep down in this big body, I'm just like anyone else. I want to be respected for who I am and what I do. This has been a lifelong struggle for me. I remember in fifth-grade gym, Mr. Harris, our teacher, used to pick on me for being the fat kid. Once, he called me out to do pull-ups in front of the entire class. He knew I couldn't do even one. I was terrified. I was humiliated.

Sometimes I wonder how different my life would have turned out had I been able to do even one pull-up. Just one.

Having been passed over at work and now reporting to Doug, it would be easy to just turn off the engine and coast along, or maybe even leave the company altogether. But, to my surprise, it's having exactly the opposite effect. It's causing me to work harder. I can't explain why. Maybe it's because I'm determined to show my colleagues that I'm just as talented and driven to succeed as they are. Or maybe, after all these years, I'm still trying to pull myself up off the ground.

In recent weeks, I've been coming into the office earlier and staying later than usual. Sometimes I work on weekends so I can keep my numbers up and prove to Chuck that he made the wrong decision. Also, I went out and bought a new Italian suit, two sizes too small. I can't even get into it! But I will. It's my incentive to lose weight. I've always wanted a nice suit, a really nice one. Now I have one, if I can just get into it. I have to. My doctor tells me I'm at risk of stroke, heart attack, diabetes, which means I have to limit my intake of red meat and bread, and eat more vegetables, more salmon with its heart-healthy omega-3s. I'm trying. But it's not easy, especially considering the hours I put in at the office. And sometimes I *need* a chicken-fried steak or a Megaburger with cheese to put things into the proper perspective. My doctor tells me I should start by eating a salad. Just once. Forego my typical cheeseburger lunch and have a grilled-salmon salad instead. But that's no easy task.

Good food is like an old friend. It's how I see the world, though I understand the corollary here is that food is also the prism through which the world views me. Even my dog, which I adopted from a local shelter at the behest of my sister, Ann, who insists that dog owners enjoy a higher quality of life, looks at me and wags his tail with the expectation of dinner, or at least a treat. I guess you'd call me the "Food Guy."

My mother always said I was a good eater. My grandmother used to say I'd eat anything that didn't eat me first. She meant this in the best possible way. And it's true. Most people eat to live. I live to eat. Why not? It's food, food, food, everywhere you look—most of it fast food, which, while lacking the nutritional value my doctor says I need, namely fiber and lean protein, certainly complements my hectic schedule and busy lifestyle. It's not ideal, but what else is there? Drinking and smoking have never appealed to me, and I have no one at home to prepare the vegetable kabobs or Mediterranean wraps or grilled-salmon salads my doctor tells me I should be eating. Not that these rabbit foods would satisfy my appetite, anyway. I need beef. I need meals with substance. I need something I can sink my teeth into and believe in.

I just don't have time to eat right, and I don't know anyone who does. Most of my life is spent at work. And if I'm not in my office working, I'm usually driving to or from work or thinking about it or answering e-mails from home. About the only time I can actually forget about my job is when I eat.

One thing's for sure: the Lord has certainly provided for me, probably too well. And when He calls me home, He's going to have to send two or three angels to carry me.

My phone rings. Now my heart's pumping and jumping, and my lungs feel like they're trying to fly away. I take a deep breath and let off the gas to put some extra distance between my car and the one in front of me. Then I glance at the phone and see Ann's name and number. The jackhammering in my chest stops. It seems I'm sliding along the highway, smooth and easy. "Hey there," I say. "For a minute I thought you were my boss."

Thanks to a highway-widening project, which bottlenecked traffic on I-44 for nearly four miles, I'm twenty minutes late getting to my doctor in Tulsa. I can't stand being late. Usually, I'm right on time. I do not miss my appointments.

By the time I park and walk into the lobby, I'm sweating and out of breath, my heart pounding so hard that the blood filling my face is causing my vision to flicker. I have to stop and rest. As I brace myself against an empty chair, heart fluttering, armpits and chest feeling clammy, an old lady in a blue smock stops and asks if I need help. I glance at her badge. Her name is Martha. She's a volunteer.

"Just heading up to Dr. Robertson's office," I tell her between breaths. "Had a long walk in. Hot out there."

"We offer a shuttle service for our patients and visitors," Martha says. "Next time, just wait for the shuttle and you won't have to work so hard."

I feel the phone in my pocket buzzing with an incoming message, then another. "Thanks," I say. "I'll remember that."

"Would you like some help getting upstairs? I can get you a wheelchair."

"That won't be necessary," I say, feeling the pressure building in my face, not only from the strain of having walked the hundred or so yards through the parking lot in ninety-degree heat, but also from embarrassment. Martha must be seventy-five years old and she's offering *me* a wheelchair.

Unsure of what else to say and still out of breath, I smile, hoping she'll leave. A second later she does, moving with the ease of a cat.

Now I gather myself and head over to the elevators. When the door opens, a doctor in a lab coat steps out and two women get in. They punch their buttons and step back, back, until they can't go any farther. As I enter the elevator, they stop talking and look down at their shoes. I know exactly what they're thinking, and I don't blame them.

Even though I'm late to my appointment, even though I'm so close to my cardiologist's office, I back out of the elevator, telling myself I'll wait for the next one.

A minute later, another elevator opens. I step inside, punch the button for the thirteenth floor, and next thing I know I'm standing at the reception desk in Dr. Robertson's office, signing in. The girl behind the desk is on the phone.

As I wait, I take in the view of the wooded, rolling hills in the distance. Now my throat feels tight, my head dizzy and light. My vision flickers. The phone in my pocket tremors with yet another message. Sometimes, I just want to throw the thing out the window.

It's a message from Karl Kassfeld, one of my clients. He's probably wondering if I've heard from the hiring manager he interviewed with two days ago. I haven't, which tells me Karl didn't get the job. Of course, this means I've missed out on another commission.

I don't know what it is with Karl. He looks great on paper, but things seem to fall apart every time he interviews. I've tried coaching him. I've tried to teach him which questions to ask a potential employer, and how much or little to say. But it hasn't worked. He's been on five interviews without an offer of employment.

It's frustrating to have to tell a client, time after time, that it just wasn't the right fit. Sometimes I tell myself there has to be an easier way to make a living.

The girl hangs up the phone. "May I help you?" she says.

I take a deep breath, realizing I must look like a madman, an extremely obese madman: hot, sweaty, flustered. "I have an eleven o'clock with Dr. Robertson," I say. "I'm a few minutes late."

The girl glances at the clock on the wall. There is a tattoo of a rose on her neck just above her shirt collar and, beside this, the faint bulge of an artery, pulsing with the commuting blood cells within. She bites her lip. She's thinking. Finally she says, "Dr. Robertson's already with another patient, so we'll probably need to reschedule you."

Anguish, dread, frustration race through my body, fighting one another as they compete for space. My heart palpitates. I've made so many sacrifices just getting here—sitting paralyzed in traffic out on the freeway; having to leave work at a time when I really need to be at my desk. Now regret joins the fray, which only complicates matters.

I do not miss my appointments.

And yet I have.

"I can wait," I say, while telling myself I really should just reschedule and get back to the office. I can almost feel my inbox piling up with requests, the pool of work swelling, Doug wondering what's taking me so long.

"He's booked solid for the rest of the afternoon," she says. "But if you want to hang out for a while, he may be able to see you. It could be a while, though. There's two ahead of you."

I glance over my shoulder at the waiting area. The loveseat on which I usually sit is taken, as are two of the room's four side chairs. These seats, obviously designed for average-size people, are separated from the loveseat by a magazine-choked coffee table, which today reminds me of the fulcrum on a seesaw: one loveseat equals four average-size chairs.

"If you'd like, you can head down to the cafeteria and get something to eat, or . . . " the girl says as she twirls a strand of her hair into a knot. "I have your cell number here, so I'll call you when the doctor's ready to see you."

How does she know I'm hungry? Is it that obvious?

The Food Guy. I tell myself I'll never be able to move beyond this. People will never see me in any other light.

The idea of hospital food doesn't appeal to me, but at least I'll be able to sit at a table where I can relax, where I won't feel so constricted. I'm grateful for that. "Thank you," I say.

I leave the office and take the elevator down to the ground floor, then follow the signs to the cafeteria, where I spot my sister Ann, and her son, Clay.

"What are you two doing here?" I say.

"Uncle Rick!" Clay says as he comes over for a hug. I love the kid. He's my favorite nephew. But sometimes I feel guilty because Ann says he looks up to me. I'm not much to look up to; or maybe I'm too much to look up to, and that's the problem. I don't want Clay to turn out like me. Already, he's a chunk. Ann says he weighs nearly a hundred pounds and he's only nine years old.

"I just got off work and picked up Clayton," Ann says. "We were right around the corner. You sounded flustered on the phone. You okay?"

"Oh, there's nothing to worry about," I tell her. "It's just a routine visit. I come in every three months," I say, glancing into the cafeteria where the scent of grilled meat is making my stomach drip. I smell chicken-fried steak, my favorite. Of course, where there's chicken-fried steak, there's bound to be cream gravy and mashed potatoes. Around here, it's a package deal. You order one and you get them all.

"Mom, can we eat?" Clay says. "I'm hungry." We follow him into the cafeteria, where he weaves through the clots of people standing in the aisle.

"Wait for us," Ann says. But Clay doesn't seem to hear her. He's heading straight for the hot-food line. My kind of kid. "You said you weren't feeling well," Ann says. "Have you been taking your blood-pressure medicine?"

We move into the food line where, behind the glass window, potatoes and green beans and steaks steam aromatically, provocatively. Clay has already worked his way ahead and he's looking at the pies and pudding in the dessert case.

"I think it was just the heat," I say. "I feel better in here."

"I *bet* you do," she says.

I glance at my sister. "That wasn't nice," I say.

"Clayton, get over here," she says, shaking her head. Then, to me she whispers, "You're here to see your doctor. You shouldn't be in the cafeteria."

That's my sister, always acting like she knows best.

"He's with someone else right now," I say. "Besides, I'm starved."

Ann snaps her fingers and raises her voice. "Clayton, get away from that case and get over here!"

Some of the others turn and look at us. Not me! I want to say. It was her! She's the bossy one.

Clay pulls himself away from the dessert case and walks over. "Mom, can we have a piece of cake?"

"You don't need any cake," she says. "We stopped by to see Uncle Rick, not to eat sweets."

I glance at the creamy potatoes and hot steaks on the other side of the window. I'm so hungry my tongue feels like it's melting.

"We never get to eat cake," Clay says.

"You don't want any cake," I say, still eyeing the chicken-fried steak and potatoes.

"See?" Ann says. "Listen to your Uncle Rick."

"Yeah, you don't want any cake," I say. "It won't fill you up. Plus, it'll make you fat, like me." He looks at me skeptically, so I pat my belly and nod my head. At this point, I'm feeling almost intoxicated by the scent of hot food. My knees feel weak. My head is spinning. And then something happens. Something inside me breaks. Snaps. Melts. I grab Clay's hand and we move out of the hot-food line. "Come on," I say, looking across the cafeteria. "Let's go get us something good."

"I don't like any of this," Clay says as we move into the salad line.

"That's because you're not eating it right," I tell him, filling his plate and mine with lettuce, tomatoes, onions, cucumber slices, carrots, and beets. "You have to eat it like a rabbit."

"A rabbit?" he says. "That's funny, Uncle Rick."

We find a table and Clay scrunches his nose when I slide his plate in front of him. I'm on my third or fourth bite. It feels like I'm eating crispy air; there's flavor, but no substance. I know this salad's going to do next to nothing to appease my appetite, and yet I can feel myself filling up. Suddenly, somehow, I'm full, filled, content, even as I continue forking the salad into my mouth. A moment later, I look over at Clay. "You ever seen a fat rabbit?" I say.

Clay looks at Ann. She grins and raises her eyebrows, then sips her tea. A moment later, a man takes a seat at the table next to us. He's wearing a very nice suit—slate gray and perfectly tailored. He squeezes a lemon wedge over the piece of fish on his plate and briefly I wonder if it's salmon. Then I look at Clay. "Have you?" I say again.

"No," Clay says, the word spilling out of his mouth like hot gravy from a ladle, slow and thick. "Uncle Rick, that's silly."

I shovel more of the salad into my mouth and chew. Then I run my hand over my head and say, "You ever see a rabbit with bad hair?"

Clay giggles and glances at Ann. "Rabbits don't have hair."

"Sure they do. They have hair," I say. "It's called fur. And it's soft and thick."

"I love rabbits," Clay says.

"Their fur is so soft and thick because they eat their rabbit food." I point to the salad. "This stuff."

"I don't like lettuce," Clay says.

"That's what rabbits eat," I say. "Lettuce and stuff. That's why they're so skinny and have good hair. And they can run fast. And jump. Plus, it tastes good."

Clay looks at Ann. He' s skeptical, I can tell. But he's grinning. I keep eating. After a while, he picks up his fork and holds it over his salad, hovering inches above a future he can't see, teetering on the edge of a great big unknown. I glance over at the man eating his lunch at the table next to us. I wonder what he does for a living. His suit's perfect.

5

Walleyed

When you've filleted stringer after stringer of fish every day for the past twenty-nine days, you just lose all interest in going fishing. All you really care about is sleeping, and making it through another day as quickly as possible so you can go home and sleep some more. This is because you're exhausted, because you've been on the water since six o'clock in the morning, and because you know that you won't be home again until long after dark. Sleep is all too brief to really be enjoyed, and before you know it, it's time to do it again. Then, because the reels need to be spooled with fresh line and because the boat needs to be gassed up and bait netted, you get out of bed and walk down the dark lake road to the dock, where bugs are still sizzling on the hot street light, and begin your day.

I'm about to wash the blood and scales from my hands, making it twenty-nine and a half, when the boss walks up the dock with a couple of morning clients. I want so badly to tell them all just to leave me alone for five minutes so that I can eat a sandwich. But I manage to keep my tongue under control, probably because the boss is smiling and waving goodbye to the couple. Catch-and-release types, I assume. Fine with me. But I bet the boss didn't like it. He says heavy stringers make for bigger tips from his customers.

He walks up to me with that big grin, slaps me on the back, and right away I know he wants something.

"Sam, how about knocking off early this afternoon and we go fishing?" he says. With his bushy gray mustache and fat, jiggling jowls, he reminds me of a walrus.

The boss never calls me by my real name, so I'm suspicious right off the bat. And why does he want me to go fishing with him? He's got lots of buddies. Besides, I'm too busy. Since he took over the lodge and guiding business my granddad used to own, I haven't had the least bit of interest in fishing. Either I'm filleting fish, or taking a tourist fishing, or doing some odd job around the docks. Why would I want to go fishing?

But it wasn't always this way.

Granddad used to take me out in his old aluminum boat and we'd listen to the woodpeckers hammering and the wood saws buzzing in the distance as we fished for walleye. He'd wear that cowboy hat, big as Texas, and smoke that pipe. He always said it kept the mosquitos away. I can still smell the cherry-blend tobacco and see the smoke billowing out from beneath his hat brim. We would fish until we had enough for dinner, then we'd take them home and fry them in corn meal. "Take all you can eat for dinner," he used to say, "but never freeze them." Granddad always told me frozen fish have no flavor and he said folks who freeze their fish are greedy. "Sam, if you have to freeze the fish you take home, you've taken too many," he'd say.

Sometimes, when I'm washing the boss' boats or filleting fish or changing lower-unit fluid, I wonder why the Lord spared me.

I'd gotten out of bed early that morning to try and catch a carp in the grassy coves on the other side of Willis Lake here in eastern Oklahoma. I noticed the smoke on the way back in, about mid-morning. By the time I reached the house, everything was charred and black, still smoldering. That was four years ago, but it seems like another life.

"What do you say?" says the boss, whose name is Bruce. He has more money than sense. I don't know how he came into it. "You want to make some dough?"

"Sure. When's the tournament?"

"Tonight. And Sly done cancelled out on me. If we win, I'll split the prize with you," he says, bringing his tattooed hand down as though it were a butcher knife halving a flank.

Everything is about the money, and that bothers me. If I had any, I would've been able to take over my granddad's business. He'd been teaching me how to guide since I was eight or nine; I'm nineteen now and I know this lake better than the boss ever will. If the tourists hadn't been so few and far between those last few years before granddad died, if he hadn't gone into debt, I could be running the business right now.

All I can manage is a "Humph," as if I've got better things to do than drag a few lures through the water in hopes of hooking into a fish big enough to buy the groceries. It sounds corny even to me, the guy with only three dollars in his pocket. And this has to last until Friday.

"Come on! What do you say, Sport?"

"Sport" is certainly a new one. The boss has called me lots of names, but never this one. I can smell alcohol on his breath so I figure it's just the beer making him say it.

I finish washing the slime and scales from my hands and then spray off the fish-cleaning table. I still haven't given him an answer, but with three dollars in my wallet, what choice do I have?

"Yeah, I'll do it," I say, wondering how I'm going to tolerate being in a boat, in such close quarters, with him.

"Starts at four," he says. "We'll fish until dark."

The thermometer at the bait shop says it's ninety degrees as we motor off from the docks. I'm sure I've fished lots of times in weather hotter and more miserable than this. I just can't remember when. We're in "Fred," one of the boss' old aluminum boats, with a twenty-five horse, tiller-drive outboard that sputters and smokes like it has emphysema. Why he gave the boat a man's name, and not a woman's, I'll never know. But that's the boss for you.

The noisy motor and oppressive heat combine to make a bad afternoon even worse. Cruising across the lake, my arms crossed, hot air blowing across my face, I let out a "Stick it!" and suddenly I feel a little better.

"Stick ups?" the boss yells from the tiller. "This time of year? You think they'll hold fish?"

"Dork!" I shout.

"I can't hear you!" he yells, never letting off the throttle. "Where?"

I hold up my arms and shake my head. "Wherever," I say.

We leave the Long Creek arm and round a gravel point, then parallel a tall rock bluff that looks white in the sunshine. Finally, we enter an arm of the lake called Coon Creek. This surprises me because the boss normally doesn't fish this part of the lake. I feel like he's coming up here somehow for my benefit, probably because this is the water I know best. This is where my family's house used to be, where I used to fish with my granddad. I can still remember the location of every ledge and shoal.

"Back of the creek?" he yells over the coughing outboard. I turn and give him a thumbs-up, nod my head. The wind, which is convection-oven warm at this hour, blows his mustache back on his cheeks, exposing his yellow teeth. For a moment, he reminds me of a weathered Viking.

We stop the boat over a hump situated in about forty feet and drop our baits to the bottom. Almost immediately, I feel a tap and set the hook. The fish shakes its head, but doesn't pull hard, which tells me it's a small one. The boss doesn't know how big it is. And because I can't stand him, I decide to mess with him.

"I think I got a big one!" I shout. I turn to look at him, eyes wide, forcing a grin. "I think he's what we're looking for."

"No kidding, Sport. Get him!" he says. He claps his hands smartly, rubs them together. "Yes sir!"

Soon, I pull a fourteen-inch walleye to the surface, shake my head. "I sure thought he was bigger than this. He felt bigger," I say.

The boss says nothing, but I can feel his disappointment, which makes me happy.

There's a protective slot limit on all walleye between thirteen and sixteen inches, so I drop the fish back into the lake, rig another minnow, and send it to the bottom. For several minutes all is calm and quiet. We sit in the boat and bake.

"Wish we had some of that shade over here," says the boss, looking at the cedars lining the shoreline. From my position the trees look like green sentries or chaperones, supervising the proceedings for everyone's best interest. Moments later, a raccoon emerges from the trees and begins policing the shoreline, shuffling its front paws through the water, feeling, withdrawing them, and repeating the process farther down the bank.

I hear a rustling noise and look back at the boss, who pulls a pistol from his bag and aims it at the raccoon.

"What the hell are you doing?" I say.

"Watch this," he says, drawing a bead on the animal.

I do the only thing I can think of, which is to rock the boat side to side in order to throw off his aim. I grab the gunwales and shift my weight back and forth to get the boat rocking. The boss shoots anyway. The sound of the shot echoes off the water's surface, scaring the raccoon, apparently unscathed, into the trees.

"What are you, a softie?" he says. "It's just a coon."

"Exactly," I say. "What did a raccoon ever do to you?"

"Come on, Sport. They're just varmints."

"We came to fish, so let's fish," I say.

The boss returns the pistol to his bag and picks up his pole. Though it's quiet and calm here on the lake, my heart is thumping. Beads of sweat roll down my temples. A couple of motorboats go racing by out in the main lake, the sounds of their outboards buzzing loudly for a moment, then growing faint. I imagine the invigorating scent of the cedars, but with no wind, all I can smell are the oil and gas from the boat's engine.

A few minutes later the sun's dimmer switch is turned down a notch as the first clouds roll into the area. About this time, I get another tap on my rod. The fish whacks the bait and the fight is on. Instantly the line is tight and weaving back and forth, slicing through the water's emerald surface. The fish feels like a kind of mild electricity being transmitted through the line, straining and pulling, bending the rod, causing the reel's drag to buzz.

The result is a twenty-two-inch walleye that sure makes the boss happy. In fact, he's so happy he just starts laughing.

"I knew you knew what you was doing over here. I'm glad you came along, Sport," he says, still laughing. Then he reaches into the cooler and draws a beer, offers. I shake my head and tell myself I'm here only because I need the money.

The boss knows I grew up on Coon Creek, and he also knows I'm familiar with the different features of this arm of the lake. But I still don't know why he asked me to come along. He's got plenty of pals who he likes to fish with, most of them silly about drinking beer, just like he is. I wish one of them would've come along instead of me. I'm still upset about him trying to shoot the raccoon.

The sky is growing darker, and after being glass-smooth only moments ago, the lake's surface is now choppy and agitated from the wind. The breeze is a welcome relief from the stifling heat and it heralds that coveted moment that anglers dream about, when the fish begin feeding prior to the arrival of a front. If you're a real fisherman, this is the time you want to be on the water.

I look back at the boss, who is taking a long pull off the bottle. He pitches the bottle cap into the lake.

I shake my head and tell myself to try and forget it. The season's almost over. Soon, I'll be cutting wood for the winter and I can forget the boss for a while. Maybe next year I'll sign on with a different outfitter. Maybe I'll start my own guiding business one of these days. Or maybe I'll move to town and get a job, and try living like everyone else for a while.

"You still got your bait?" he says. "Check your bait, boy."

I reel in the hook, lift it out of the water where he can see the wiggling minnow. He nods, and I drop it back into the deep.

"How about yours?" I ask. "You haven't checked yours in a while."

"Mine's fine. Just catch us another one, Tiger."

Moments later, I hear the sound of another outboard, and I look to see a small boat cruising into the creek. The boat doesn't keep its distance; rather, it approaches closer and closer. Now I recognize the vessel and its captain. It's Sly, the boss' fishing buddy and fellow outfitter, whose real name is Sylvester.

I turn around and look at the boss. "I thought Sly wasn't fishing," I say.

"What's old Sly doing?" he says, ignoring my question. "He got that boy driving him around?"

"No, Sly's at the tiller," I tell him. Sometimes, I wonder if the boss needs glasses.

The black dot at the bow is none other than Sly's laborer, Toussaint, and as the boat approaches I hold up two fingers. Toussaint, or "Two," as I call him, is one of the few people around the lake who I have any respect for. He works his ass off, as hard or harder than me, and for less money. He's even got a wife and two kids at home. He's about the only friend I've got around here, and he knows the lake, knows it better than the boss or Sly. I taught him.

Sly lets off the throttle as the boat swings in close, its wake causing us to bob up and down like a buoy. "You going to be netting anything today?" he says with a grin.

"Got one keeper about twenty-two," says the boss. "You?"

Sly shakes his head. I really want to tell the boss that he needn't ask this question, because if an angler is having any luck then he stays put. The ones who aren't catching anything are the ones you see running all across the lake. My granddad taught me that.

"What's going on, Two?" I say, trying to have a conversation of my own. He and I stick together because we must be the only two stupid enough to hire out to guys like the boss and Sly. And if there was anything else to do around here, I think we would've split by now and found an easier way to make a living.

Two shakes his head, wrinkles his brow. "Man, if I had more notice that I was going fishing I'd have brought some real drink. Not this Rhineland beer crap. Stuff taste like pine needles."

At this, Sly, who wears a beard in order to cover a scar on his cheek, turns and glares at Two. "I said I'd split the prize money with you if we win. But you haven't found shit. You want to get paid, you got to find the fish."

Then Sly trains his dark eyes on me. There's an Arkansas Razorbacks cap cocked back on his head, and a tattered gray T-shirt draped over his skinny frame. "A good guide should be able to put his clients on fish," he says, looking from me to Two. "Where's the fish?"

I know Sly's remark is intended for Two. I also know it wouldn't be worth the hardship, but I sure wish Two would just pop that skinny old coot right in the mouth, put him in the lake. Two's solid. One punch is all it would take. But he has bills to pay, like me. So he keeps his mouth shut.

A rush of cool air hits us just as Sly and Two motor off. It feels like cool lake water on your body when you jump off the dock. It smells like water and dirt, and for a moment it's invigorating. Then exhaust fumes from Sly's outboard attack my lungs, and I hold my breath until they pass.

The sky has turned purple to the northwest and slate gray to the east. Thunder rumbles as the boss reels in his hook, which I notice is bare.

"Where to, Sport?" he asks, twisting open another beer. "You say where and we'll get there."

I shrug my shoulders. Though I haven't fished this creek in probably three years, I know there's a long point tapering off into the channel a few hundred yards west of here. On the lower end of this point is a stump bed and the area always holds fish. It's especially good for big fish. But I'm not telling the boss. After seeing Sly and Two, I know he's up to something. He wants to win the tournament and that prize money like he always does. I'm not sure how he does it, but he always seems to win. This time, I'm going to see if I can help him lose.

"Let's go back out to the mouth," I tell him.

"Mouth? Don't you think they'll be moving shallow with these clouds?"

"Nah. I think the mouth is the place we need to hit," I say. "We're going to have to hurry. Sky's getting pretty dark."

"We've got over three hours yet," he says, cranking the engine. Before motoring off, he pulls a rain suit from one of his bags and slips it on. I'm angry with myself for forgetting mine, and for having to ask to borrow one.

"This is the only one I got, Sport," he says. "Wish I'd thought to bring a spare. This rain'll probably move through pretty quick, though. We might not even get wet."

I know this isn't the case. I know I'm going to get wet.

"Sniff them out, Sport," says the boss, a cigar wedged into the corner of his mouth. After idling around the mouth of the creek for several minutes, I motion for him to stop, tell him that this looks like a good spot, though I know it's completely featureless beneath the surface. Rain begins falling as soon as we put our baits in the water. It progresses from sprinkles to a solid, soaking rainfall in minutes. The temperature seems to have dropped twenty degrees.

"Come on," I yell over the noise of the rain. "Fish aren't biting. Let's go back."

"To hell with that," comes the response from beneath the rain suit. "This is the best weather for catching fish. We just have to find them."

"I don't think they're going to bite. There's fish all over here and we would've caught one by now," I say. "Let's go home. I'm soaked anyway."

Then, as if a giant hatch has been opened somewhere up in the sky, the rain begins falling in heavy, solid layers. The water's surface is alive with tiny white droplets, flickering as far as I can see. Fishing is out of the question. I reel in my hook and drop the rod. I'm wet. I'm cold. I'm finished.

At dusk, it's still raining. Sitting in the bow on the way in, cold and shivering, my sopping clothes permanent fixtures to my clammy skin, I feel the boat swerving. I look back at the boss and there he is, walleye in one hand, lead steroids in the other, dropping the weights into the fish's mouth, poking them in with his finger. With his rain hood pulled down over his head, he doesn't see me, but I turn back around, anyway. I feel a fire burning in my stomach, even though I'm cold and wet. People like the boss are a different breed.

The lead weights are his insurance policy. He's going to make sure he wins this tournament. But why? He has plenty of money, a big truck, a nice house. Why is it so important for him to win these tournaments for a few hundred dollars? I've never liked the boss, but I always thought it was because of the circumstances of how we met, him buying my granddad's old business and all. Now I know why I can't stand him.

Ours is the fourth boat to reach the dock and we have only a single walleye to weigh in. The boss grins as he hoists the fish into the air for the others to see. There is a collective groan from the other anglers; apparently their luck hasn't been so good.

Sly and Two are already there, standing back from the edge of the dock, beneath the bait shop's awning. Like me, Two is dripping wet. I duck under the awning, thankful to be out of the rain, and someone hands me a paper cup. The smell of coffee and cigarettes, and the coffee cup's warmth on my fingers, are like luxuries after being out on the water. I watch as another pair of anglers walks up the dock, empty-handed, heads drooping.

Two turns and says, "Remind me again why my ass ain't out in California where it's warm."

"No kidding," I say. "If you ever go, take me with you."

Sly is beaming as the boss puts the fish to scales. He reminds me of the carnival attendant who situates his bottles in such a way that the lightweight ball will never knock them over, or the one who coats his balloons with a thin layer of lacquer, which helps to deflect the dull-tipped darts.

"Five-two. No, five-three," says Bernard, the owner of the bait shop. He looks warm and comfortable in his plaid Mackinaw jacket. I've always liked Bernard, but now I wonder if he's in on the boss' scam. It makes me sad to see these dozen or so anglers here on the docks. They've endured the weather to come out and fish, while the boss cheats his way to a paycheck. "Not bad," Bernard says, "but I figured the fishing would be a lot better with this system moving in."

The boss looks at me, then glances at Sly, who's still grinning.

The covered space beneath the awning is completely full as the crowd waits for the other teams to weigh their catches. One guy is already at the ramp, trailering his boat, while several more are leaving the docks, rain hoods covering their heads.

I sip the coffee, listen to the rain drumming the bait shop's tin roof, watch it falling through the illuminated space above the dock. I'm exhausted, hungry, disgusted. There's really no use in me staying around because I know who's going to win the tournament. It was decided long before Bernard put the fish on the scales. But it doesn't concern me and I couldn't care less. I'm just going to slip off and go home, put on some dry clothes and forget about all this. And I'll keep my mouth shut because I need the money. Tomorrow makes thirty-one days.

6

Confluence

It was the second Saturday in April. Our annual spring blow-out. Prices slashed on last year's merchandise to make room for the latest and greatest. Out with the old, in with the new.

Customers pawed through the racks and rooted through the bins. Near the open double doors, bees buzzed around tins of empty sodas while neglecting the planters of flowers and their fragrant blooms.

Big Frank had his food truck set up out front and people were making U-turns in the middle of the street to get back to our place for one of his famous fish tacos, which he served out of an old RV that had once been used to transport hot-air-balloon enthusiasts across the country and whose side panels still featured a rainbow of the colorful aircraft ascending into a cloudless blue sky. It was curious branding for a taco truck. Perhaps even misleading. But people said one savory bite would hook you and pull you away to some happy place where you'd understand how real love tasted.

I'd never tried them, so I was skeptical. But I didn't need to. I was a fly fisherman. I spent upward of two hundred days a year on the water and tied all my own flies. And twice during the throes of my passion—that is, while fishing the blue-winged olive hatch, casting to rising trout—I had hooked, fought, and landed personal-best fish of twenty-four and, later, twenty-six, inches, which incited in me such a surge of primal emotion that I snatched blue-winged olive duns out of the air and popped them into my mouth like jellybeans, their bittersweet flavor lingering on my tongue long after I'd swallowed them.

Not a typical response to an insect hatch, I realize, but I'd been compelled to eat those BWO duns, which were my favorite of all mayflies. Call it a crime of the heart.

Or maybe I was a trout in another life.

In any event, I already knew the flavor of true love. And because of this, I didn't have to stand in line at Big Frank's taco truck. Well, that and the fact that there were people on the casting yard who needed my assistance.

Factory representatives from all the major fly-rod companies were on hand that day so customers could try out the latest graphite sticks. Our casting yard was packed, which delighted Floyd, my boss, who said we needed the business. He was in and out of the store, sipping coffee, helping customers find just the right rod or reel, while I patrolled the casting yard, bullshitting with the factory reps and giving casting demonstrations.

When I came upon a woman who seemed mesmerized by the flex of the fly rod in her hand, I stood back and observed her. She had frizzy brown hair and wore a pair of loose-fitting jeans, which concealed her figure. Except for her nails, which were painted sky blue, she looked rather plain and earthy. Not my type. But she had a fly rod in her hand and looked like she could use a few pointers, so I was intrigued.

Mark, the factory rep who'd been assisting her, saw me and shook his head. Either he'd made a pass at her and she'd shot him down, or her inability to cast was making her self-conscious and snippy. Maybe both.

A moment later, the woman got her line tangled with the man beside her.

"Let me help," I said, grabbing the two lines. Every time this happened—on our casting yard it happened all the time, especially on Saturdays when it was crowded—my mind flashed back to childhood, to getting my fishing lure caught in a tree or on a snag and having to ask my pop for help. Sometimes he would be across the pond and I'd have to shout to get his attention, which always pissed him off because he said I was scaring the fish. But he would walk over and help me, anyway, even though I knew he hadn't wanted to stop fishing, even though I might have just asked for his help ten minutes before and likely would have to ask again a few minutes later.

"This is a lot harder than it looks," the woman said. She didn't seem frustrated or disappointed; she was just making an observation.

I untangled the lines and let them fall to the ground, one on either side of me. The man retrieved his and moved away without a word. I turned to the woman. "It's really not," I said. "If I can do it, anybody can do it."

"That's good to hear," she said. "But I—"

"Go ahead and fire one out there. Let me see what you got."

"Not much. I'm not a natural caster," she said, heaving the rod backward, then jerking forward, causing a series of waves in the line. It looked like one of those jagged fissures that opens up in the parched earth when a lake goes dry, when it seems an eternity has passed without water. What I wanted to see was a smooth, straight line. But I could fix that.

"I've taught lots of people to cast. I can teach you, too."

"Do you teach women to cast?"

"All the time," I said. "Take in a little more of that line."

"Women like me?"

What was this supposed to mean? Regardless, I was sharper than she gave me credit for, and college-educated, even if I was working in a fly shop for ten dollars an hour. According to my wife, Quincy, this was part of the problem. I couldn't have disagreed more. It's not that I lacked ambition. It's just that I wanted no part of the hypoxic corporate world, which seemed so alluring to everyone else. I knew I'd never be able to pay off my student loans, but I loved working around people who spoke my language. The language of fishing.

Quincy didn't get it. In five years of marriage, she never had, which was part of the reason why we were estranged.

Evidently, this woman did get it. At least, I thought so. She had a fly rod in her hand and wanted to learn how to cast. This was further than I ever got with Quincy.

"All kinds of women," I said. "Even some with pretty brown eyes."

She smiled and said, "You probably say that to all the girls." Then she said, "I'm Leslie, by the way."

"Name's Travis," I said, shaking her hand, searching her face, trying to decide if we'd met. She looked familiar.

More customers were crowding around the casting yard, trying new rods, cracking jokes, and laughing. There were lots of smiles. Casting a fly rod has that effect on people. It's a cathartic process, and even if you aren't very good, it's still a privilege to hold a fine rod in your hand and feel it flex under the tension of the line as you wave it back and forth. It's the closest thing I can think of to holding a magic wand.

There must have been two dozen of us out there firing fly lines toward the street as if the pavement were a river, as if the cars zipping by were rainbow trout, as if we didn't need hooks to make a catch. There were people casting on either side of us and I regretted being so cramped because I knew how tricky it was learning to cast in such close quarters. But a moment later the man to our left reeled in his line and left the casting yard, offering up valuable space, which I fully intended to take advantage of. I was about to tell Leslie to move down when another caster—a slender, older woman in khaki slacks and a safari shirt—appeared, filling the void. She had a smooth, effortless casting style and a healthy tan, which told me she'd done this before.

I was afraid Leslie was going to get her line tangled a second time. Then, very subtly, she began inching her way to the right and I knew then the earlier lesson on tangled lines hadn't been lost on her. She was learning.

Still, her form needed a great deal of refinement. But I told myself I could fix that.

"Stop your arm up high on the backcast," I said.

She made another cast, but now she dropped her shoulder and moved her elbow, which created waves in the fly line.

"A little more speed on the forward stroke," I said.

"This is really technical," she said. "I didn't realize there was so much to it."

"After a while, it just becomes natural," I said. "Like drinking coffee in the morning."

"Or Red Bull?" she said.

"Or Red Bull," I said.

Her speech had taken on the cadence of her casting: a few words on the forward cast, a pause, then another rapid-fire statement on the backcast. "This is fun," she said, watching her line unfold, "but I wish I was better."

"You're doing fine," I said. "Try keeping your elbow close to your body."

"How close?"

I gently grabbed her elbow and tucked it in beside her torso, then removed my hand. There was nothing unusual or overtly forward about this. I did it all the time. With casting ergonomics, some respond better to being shown.

So why did I feel the bite of excitement when I grabbed her elbow? Why was my heart skipping? I tried to ignore what I was feeling. The last thing I needed was to hook up with a new woman when I was trying to wriggle free from someone else. In fact, I was still saving to pay for my divorce, which are quite expensive in California and which are almost cost-prohibitive for someone on my career track. But I was determined.

Still, it felt like Leslie and I were suddenly tethered together with a fishing line and someone was turning the reel, pulling us closer, tighter. Maybe she felt it, too, because her next cast flew straight out and the line unfolded beautifully before she snapped the rod back.

"There!" I said. "Did you see the difference that made?"

"I think so."

"Did you feel it? Did you feel the way the rod bent, the way the line shot out?"

"I can't say I did, Travis. This is all so new to me."

"So, what brings you out today? You planning a trip somewhere?"

"Not really," she said, her words mirroring the motion of the rod in her hand. "I've been wanting to learn fly casting for a long time, so I thought I'd stop by. It seemed fun."

I glanced around the casting yard, wondering if I should move on and assist someone else. But Leslie was unique. She was easily the worst caster in the yard, which meant she had much more opportunity for improvement than anyone else. And for whatever reason, maybe because it was my job, I wanted to help this girl. So I told myself to stay put. "What do you think?" I said. "Is it fun?"

"I'm loving it," she said. "But unfortunately I have to run to the office."

"You can come back anytime. We teach casting every day," I said. "Hey, while you're here, you may as well enter your name in our raffle. We're giving away all kinds of stuff."

"Sure."

I placed the rod in the rack and as we headed across the casting yard a man standing nearby said something that jarred my memory, reminding me where I'd seen Leslie.

"Eight hundred bucks?" he said. "If I brought this home, I'd have to turn right around and go see a divorce lawyer."

"Now I know where I've seen you," I said. "You're a lawyer."

Leslie grinned.

"I've seen your face somewhere. Maybe on a billboard? Or the evening news."

"I'm fairly certain you haven't seen me on the evening news," she said. "At least I hope you haven't."

"You a divorce lawyer?"

"I am," she said. "You know anyone looking to cut the knot, have them give me a call."

"Actually, I'm in the market," I said.

"Well, I guess it's meant to be," she said. "Let me get you my card."

She opened the door to an olive-green Prius and leaned inside. "Call my office and schedule a consultation. It's free."

"I appreciate it, but I'm not sure I can afford—"

"Call me anyway," she said. "I've enjoyed talking to you. You remind me of someone I used to know."

"Well, you remind me of someone I've seen on a billboard. Or was it the evening news?"

"Ha!" she said, tapping my arm with the back of her hand. Then her cell phone rang. "I have to take this. Can you go ahead and register me?"

"Will do," I said.

She waved. "See you soon, Travis!"

I climbed the steps to the shop, watching her pull out into the street, where she merged into traffic and disappeared like a mayfly in the breeze.

I met my wife during my junior year at UCLA. She was from Virginia, where her parents still lived and where her father, Don, was a State Farm agent. Not long after we met, Quincy found out I had a liability policy with State Farm on the old Honda I was driving and she commented that I'd made a smart choice in insurance. Maybe I had, but I was also a hungry college student and money was elusive. Eventually, circumstances dictated that I choose between insurance and food and electricity. Sometimes, I found myself having to decide whether to pay my insurance premium or use that money for my next fishing trip. Naturally, I allowed my policy to lapse. I drove without insurance for nearly six months before Quincy found out, and when she did we nearly broke up.

"How can you drive around like you're covered when you're not?" she'd said.

I laughed at her, trying to downplay the situation. "Because my stomach told me to," I said.

Quincy wanted to follow her parents into the insurance industry. Her dream was to become a State Farm agent, and she was always telling me how great it would be to run a franchise together and spend our careers being the good neighbors people turned to in times of need.

But she couldn't fool me. I knew what motivated her. I knew what turned her on. "You mean you want to be the one who collects their monthly premiums when they pay their bills," I'd said to her once. She replied by rolling her eyes and telling me that everyone needed insurance.

"Not everyone," I said. "What about those who don't own homes or cars? Different people have different needs."

After graduation she landed a job as an actuary out in Riverside, in what is known here in California as the Inland Empire. The desert is not my native habitat. I was born in Oklahoma. When I was seven my family moved to the Santa Cruz area, on the central California coast. I must have spent every day surfing until I went away to college. Then it was like I never had. I met Quincy, and my priorities changed. Gradually, I changed, too.

We got married, and as she began climbing the corporate ladder, I realized I wanted off it. I had been working in customer service for a rental car company, but being tethered to a cubicle, staring at a computer screen for eight hours a day, just wasn't working out. I felt like a caged animal.

To relax from the corporate-induced stress, I didn't smoke or drink. I went fishing. I'd head to Pyramid Lake or over to San Diego, where I'd go out on one of the overnight tuna vessels. I'd always felt most at home in the outdoors, especially in or around water. I guess this is why I got into fly fishing my sophomore year. To tell you the truth, if I hadn't found it, I don't know if I would've made it through college. It was how I relaxed and recharged. There were only so many hours of books and lectures I could take before I had to get away to the water.

Even then, Quincy saw my obsession with fly fishing as a flaw, but somehow she tolerated it.

Although she never said so, I believe she thought she could change me, fix me, convert me into someone like her. But that was never going to happen. I needed fishing as much as she wanted money, and in that sense, we were like oil and water. We mixed for a time, but it didn't take long for us to separate into our respective viscosities.

Looking back, it wasn't our divergent ambitions that sunk Quincy and me; it was simply a lack of common interests. Maybe if we'd shared a hobby, or if we enjoyed, I don't know, cooking or organic foods, for example, things may have worked out differently. That's the one lesson my failed marriage taught me: a potential spouse or partner should be more than just a lover; she should also be a friend.

Things really began unraveling for us when I announced, after returning home from a fishing trip one Sunday evening, that I wanted nothing more to do with the corporate world or working in an office or wearing a suit and tie. (This was the trip on which I'd caught my first really big rainbow trout, the twenty-four-incher, and I was still feeling the rush of having eaten my first blue-winged olive mayfly, both of which had led me to this epiphany and contributed, in no small part, to this liberating promulgation.) Fly fishing was what I loved and I was going to pursue a career path in this field and see where it led me. It was the right thing for me.

The next day, I stopped at Floyd's fly shop and he hired me on the spot.

Career-wise, I'd never been happier. But Quincy didn't approve. She told me I was becoming a chronic underachiever and she didn't like the fact that I preferred to spend my weekends on the water. But how else was I going to cast a fly to rising trout or strip streamers for lunker largemouth? I used to ask Quincy if she wanted to go with me, but she always turned me down. Eventually, I stopped asking.

When Floyd called me into his office one Friday afternoon a few months later and told me he was cutting my hours because of the ongoing recession, I considered taking another part-time job to make up the difference. Only no one was hiring. It seemed everyone was reducing staff or hours, or in some cases, both. Determined to succeed in my new career, however, and adamant that I wasn't going back to a corporate job, I did the only thing I could think of. I began guiding other anglers in my off hours, helping them catch fish in the lakes and rivers I knew best. Consequently, I spent even more time on the water and away from home.

Quincy never asked me to give it up; I guess by this point she knew. We just drifted apart, she going downstream with everyone else, and me with my nose pointed upriver, fighting the current like a salmon.

The law office was situated on the edge of a suburban business park. It was a newer building with a clean, contemporary design—all angles, edges, and opaque glass—and it seemed out of place among the surrounding trees.

Leslie's secretary was a middle-aged woman named Darcy, who wore a gray suit and whose chiseled features seemed to suggest that she was carved out of granite. I was afraid of angering her because she looked like she was having a bad day. So when she told me to have a seat, I took a seat. Quickly. While I waited, I flipped through a copy of *Time*.

At one point, I glanced up from the magazine to see Darcy scowling at me from her desk.

Was it something I'd said? I wondered. All I'd said at that point was *Hi, I'm Travis Billings here to see Leslie Palomino.*

A few minutes later she stood and, without saying so, indicated that I was to follow her. So that's exactly what I did. I followed her down the hallway and into Leslie's small office, which, as Darcy closed the door, felt very much like a refuge.

"Travis!" Leslie said when I walked in, as if we were old friends. She came around the desk and hugged me. "Want something to drink?"

"Got any Red Bull?"

"I've got a refrigerator full of it. That's about all I drink," she said. "Let me get Darcy to bring you one."

"I'm kidding," I said. "Hey, thanks for getting me in today."

"That's what I'm here for," she said, grinning. She wore a loose-fitting white blouse, which hid her figure, and very little, if any, makeup. Her nails were painted blue and, as before, there was no ring on her finger. I wouldn't have called Leslie pretty, but I found her immensely attractive and part of the reason was her incandescent personality. Her brown eyes were spring-creek clear and bright as a full moon, and with her enthusiasm and energy she seemed to buzz with life. After being married to a pessimist for five years, this was exhilarating.

She looked at her computer and began typing. "Been fishing lately?"

"Not for myself," I said. "I do a little guiding on the side, so I get out on the water regularly, but it's not the same as fishing for pleasure," I said. "I'm using all my fishing money to save for this divorce. I still don't know if I can afford to pay your fee, so I don't want to waste your time."

"Don't worry about it," she said. "This is a free consultation, anyway. You sure you don't want anything to drink?"

"No, thanks," I said. "I'm too nervous to drink."

She closed her laptop, shoved it aside, and leaned back in her seat. "Why? You don't have to be nervous with me."

"Lawyers always make me nervous. I never know what it's going to cost me when I'm around them."

"There's more to life than worrying about money," she said.

"I agree with you, but a lot of people don't see it that way," I said. "My boss is one of them."

"They make me nervous, too," she said. "But it's only my day job. Underneath it all, I'm still just a girl trying to make it in this world." Then, her face serious, her brown eyes locked onto mine, she said, "Hey, you and me? We're on the same page."

"Sure, Captain. Whatever you say."

She laughed, which gave me a certain feeling about her. Although I'd just met her the week before, I could feel an unmistakable attraction to Leslie—one that reached much deeper than with most girls. For some reason, I felt a strong spiritual connection to her. Was this all because she was interested in fly fishing? I told myself that was a ludicrous idea. But it was certainly possible.

There were diplomas on the wall from the University of Nevada, Las Vegas and Arizona State, and on the credenza behind her desk were several framed photos. One was a portrait of a thin, almost gaunt, woman with beautiful blue eyes and dark hair. Her mother? The other was a black-and-white photo of a man wearing a hat and fly fishing vest. He was standing in a river with a fly rod tucked beneath his arm, holding a nice-sized trout.

Leslie took a drink from the Red Bull can on her desk. "So, how long have you and your wife been separated?"

Now a fly appeared and began buzzing around my head. "About six months," I said, swatting at the insect. "Almost seven."

Leslie eyed the fly with the focus of a predator and for a moment I thought she might grab a magazine or a newspaper and go after it. But then the insect disappeared and she returned her attention to me. "Do you own your home?" she asked.

"I rent."

"Any children?"

"No children."

"Are you contesting for anything?" she asked. She was taking notes as we talked.

"Just my walking papers," I said. "And my fly rods. She wouldn't want those," I said. "You know, I thought I'd feel pretty bad about all this. When I got married, I never thought I'd be getting a divorce someday. Then again, it never occurred to me that I might be marrying the wrong girl, either. But to tell you the truth I feel better than I've felt in a long time."

"I understand exactly how you feel," she said. "So, no real property. No children. This shouldn't be any big deal."

I scooted to the edge of my seat. "Good," I said. "Now let's talk about your fee."

"Let's talk fly casting," she said. "That sounds much more interesting. Don't you think?"

"Sure."

She leaned forward and placed her hands on her desk, fingers interlocked. "How long do you think it'll take me to learn to cast a fly rod? I want to be able to cast really well."

"Depends," I said. "You were improving the other day and you were only there for a little while. The more you practice. You know how that goes."

"Do you think you could teach me by July?"

"I know I could," I said. "That's three months from now. You got a trip planned?"

"No, but I'm thinking about planning one. I turn thirty in July and for my thirtieth birthday I want to go to Oregon and stand in the Deschutes River and cast a fly rod."

"Sounds fun," I said.

"Have you been there?"

"I wish. The Deschutes is a blue-ribbon river. I think they also get summer-run steelhead up there."

"I don't know anything about that," she said.

"You ever fished for trout?"

"No, I haven't," she said. "Look. I know how important fishing is to you, so don't take this the wrong way, but I don't want anything to do with catching a fish."

But she'd stopped by the fly shop last week, I told myself. And she wants to learn to cast. What's she talking about?

I sat back in the chair and rested my right leg on my left knee. "You don't?"

"No. I don't," she said. "I understand why people like to fish. My grandfather loved to fish. He was a passionate fly fisherman." She spun in her seat and grabbed the photo of the man holding the trout. "This is him," she said. "On his thirtieth birthday. Taken on the Deschutes River in Oregon."

"So, you want to retrace his footsteps?" I said. "You writing a memoir or something?"

Her head rolled back in laughter. "No. Nothing like that. I don't think anyone would want to read about my life," she said. "See, my grandfather was like a father to me. My mother died when I was young. Cancer. Then, when I was eleven, my father gave up on us and walked away, so my sister and I lived with my grandparents. My grandfather started this law firm in the sixties and passed it on to me when he retired. He's the reason I went into law. If it hadn't been for him, I may have ended up on the street, struggling to get by. No home, no food, no resources. The

Deschutes River was a special place for him, so I want it to be a special place for me. I want to see what he saw and feel what he felt. You know?"

I nodded and thought of Quincy's father, Don, and how she wanted to follow in his footsteps as a State Farm agent. My pop was an electrician. Growing up, I didn't know exactly what I wanted to do with my life, but I knew I didn't want to go into his line of work. Electricity scared the hell out of me. But he was also an angler, so I guess that means I followed his example in one way.

"Why don't you want to catch a fish?" I said. "Looks like your granddad used to catch trout."

"He caught fish all over the country. All over the world," Leslie said, as she looked at the photo in her hands. She placed it back on the credenza and turned around to face me. "He loved fly fishing. That was his thing. But when he would come home from a trip, he didn't talk so much about the fish he caught. He talked more about how it felt to go to these beautiful places and cast his fly rod. That was what he was after. It was like a spiritual experience for him."

"He's right. There's something special about it," I said. "There's something magical in holding a fine, American-made fly rod in your hands and casting it. It's like the rod comes alive, and you can feel it. You can feel its soul, if it has one. Some rods don't. Every rod has a different personality, you know."

"I suppose, but all that's beyond me right now," she said. "He left me his fly-rod collection. I must have two dozen rods and I can't cast any of them. That's why I want to learn. But I don't want to catch a fish. They're too pretty to catch."

"They're too pretty to ignore," I said. "But that's fine. I bet you'll change your mind."

Now the fly reappeared and began circling over the desk. Suddenly, and with astounding quickness and precision, Leslie snatched the fly out of the air. Then, with the insect trapped in her closed fist, she stood, walked to the window, lifted it open and flung it outside, then closed the window. It was all very smooth, as if she did this sort of thing several times a day. I didn't know what to say. Her efficiency and decisiveness surprised me.

"You made that look easy," I said. "Who needs a fly swatter?"

"I can't stand them in my office," she said. "They're distracting."

I laughed, feeling certain there was much more where this had come from and now wondering what other surprises she might have in store. "So you want me to teach you to cast?" I asked. "If you're willing," she said. "I could handle your case, and you could help me learn to cast. What do you think?"

"I'd love to," I said. I stood from the desk and extended my hand. She waved my hand away, then came around the desk and hugged me. "I'm a hugger. Can you tell?"

"I am, too, and I feel like I haven't had anybody to hug in a long time."

She frowned the kind of frown that made me smile. "Let's go casting and forget our problems," she said as we moved toward the door.

"I've never taught anyone to cast who didn't also want to catch a fish," I said. "You'll be my first."

"Good. You'll always remember me then."

"After seeing you catch that fly, I don't think there's any way I could forget you."

The first two lessons with Leslie were at the fly shop, but due to my abbreviated schedule, which had me on site for only twenty hours a week, we began meeting at a park a few blocks away. There was a large pond patrolled by a cacophonous fleet of ducks and an expansive, grassy lawn fringed by gardens popping with colorful flowers and humming with insects. It felt good to be standing in the sunshine beside Leslie. As she casted, we talked about all sorts of things.

By the end of the second week of lessons, Leslie was throwing fifty feet consistently. We began working on loop control, which would open up all sorts of new possibilities. Slowly, we were getting to know one another and my concerns about hanging out with a lawyer began to subside. Leslie put me at ease with her disarming laughter and her laidback personality. She seemed very genuine; she was who she was, and she didn't try to hide it or put on any pretenses. I liked that about her.

Since that day in her office, we hadn't talked about her aversion to catching a fish, but I began to believe that with just a little more time I could bring her around. If she was willing to cast a fly rod, and she was, then she couldn't resist the pull of a wild fish. I'd see to that.

Weeks passed. By early June, Leslie was casting so well that she no longer needed my instruction. Still, every time we met, I would point out some technical matter that, if mastered, would help her cast farther, easier, better. Truthfully, I was just afraid that if she felt she no longer needed my instruction, I'd never see her.

Even though she was a busy lawyer, she'd canceled only once. I found this encouraging because it told me how focused she was on learning to cast. It also suggested that she enjoyed spending time together as much as I did. Well, that's what I wanted to believe.

One unsettled, overcast evening, Leslie did everything right and I watched the line sail away from us like never before. Her loop was still tight at sixty feet and was tracking straight and fast at seventy before unfolding and falling to the ground just shy of the eighty-foot mark, despite a gusty sidewind.

"You did it!" I said, turning to her, holding my arms up.

"Thank you," she said, hugging me. Then I felt her lips peck my cheek.

Well, this is a start, I told myself. This is how it begins. All because I'd taught her to cast. I was proud of myself.

"This calls for a celebration," I said. I hadn't planned on suggesting this. It just came out.

"It does?"

"I'll buy you a drink. That's the least I can do for a cast like that."

"I shouldn't."

"Just a quick beer. There's a place I know right around the corner."

She looked off across the park as she considered it. "I guess there is a lot we need to celebrate," she said. "Your divorce will be finalized soon. Me learning to cast. Our friendship."

"So, let's go have a beer," I said.

"I'll go have a drink with you," she said. "As friends."

As friends. I dreaded hearing these words, even though I knew how important and valuable they were. It's just that, by this point, I was feeling more than friends. Much more. "You're seeing someone?" I said.

"No," she said as she studied my face. Then she looked away. "I was seeing someone, but not anymore."

"I know," I said. "You can't date your clients."

"It's not that," she said. "Look, Travis, I'm just not ready to dive into a personal relationship right now. I was burned once before and I'm still trying to deal with that."

"In fly fishing we call that being 'leader-shy'," I said. "When a fish has been hooked too many times, it gets leader shy and very hard to catch."

"You have a funny way of turning everything back to fishing."

"What else is there?" I said. She gave me this look, which made me smile.

We were sitting now on a bench, overlooking the park, watching the ducks chase each other into the water. To our left was a bed of flowers, some in full bloom, some just beginning to sprout from the earth.

"Sometimes I think I had gills in another life," I said.

She smiled and said, "I think you still do." Then she leaned over and hugged me. We sat there in silence for a long time, our arms around each other. Her hair smelled faintly of licorice. Then she stood. "I really should be going. I have some work I need to finish," she said. "We'll have that drink one of these days."

"Sure," I said.

"You're not upset with me, are you?"

I picked up the rod and we started toward the cars. "Heck no. I understand," I said. "I'm a bit leader-shy myself."

Out over the pond, mayfly duns were emerging and drifting up into the air, where the breeze scattered them like dandelion seeds. Seeing them, my mind flashed back to the day I'd caught my first big rainbow trout, a day I had something to celebrate, and yet no one to celebrate with. I recalled, afterward, eating the blue-winged olive mayfly, alone.

A moment later, one of the duns floated by, close enough to touch. Then came two more. Seeing their tiny wings fluttering as they struggled against the breeze seemed to trigger something within me, and instantly, without thinking about it, I snatched one of the flies out of the air and popped it into my mouth.

Leslie stopped and turned to me. "Did you just eat that mayfly?" she said. Her hand was gripping my forearm.

"How'd you know it's a mayfly?" I said. "Could've been a caddis."

"But it wasn't," she said. "You can tell by the wings."

"You know that?" I said. I couldn't believe what I was hearing. Was I dreaming? "How'd you know that?" I said.

She smiled. "My grandfather taught me about aquatic insects. I mean, I'm no entomologist, *but I know my bug basics, boy!*" she said. We laughed.

Now there was a cloud of white mayflies drifting by in the breeze and Leslie reached out and caught one as easily as she'd caught the fly that day in her office. Then she popped it into her mouth, smiling as she chewed.

"Show off," I said.

"I couldn't make a living eating them," she said, "but this isn't a bad way to celebrate our day."

"One of these days I'll have you catching a fish," I said. "It's in your blood."

She seemed to relax as she looked at me, grinning. "Maybe I already have," she said.

7

Something to Hold On To

When the package store calls, Wishbone always answers. Same time every afternoon. Pint bottle of whatever brand of scotch is on sale. Handed to him inside a brown paper bag, which Cinco, the manager, wraps with a couple layers of duct tape. Makes a good grip. And an hour later, with the night to look forward to, his problems are forgotten.

The package store is calling and Wishbone is on his way over when his phone rings. He pulls it from his pocket, thinking it's the girl whose apartment he just left. It's the other. She's called three times in the last hour. She'll just keep calling, he thinks. "Hey."

"It had a plus sign and it turned pink," the girl says.

"What does that mean?"

"That means I'm pregnant."

"All right, then."

"That all you got to say?"

"I gotta go," he says, ending the call. He wraps his hand around the phone, squeezing the device as if this will change the news. She's crazy, he tells himself. That baby's not mine.

He wishes he could keep driving, right out of town, go somewhere where no one knows him, where he could start over. But he knows he'll never leave Cotton County, never leave this tiny town, these blackjack-studded fields, the silty Red River and its sandy, shifty, catfish-slimed banks. It's home. Floods and all. He knows every pothole on every street in this blighted neighborhood. He knows every bullet hole in every stop sign, and the names of those who put them there. That's what happens when you spend all your life in the same small town. Like his mother and grandmother did. Like his brothers and sisters will.

He wonders for a moment what his father is doing these days, or if he's still alive.

Soon, he rolls to a stop in front of the package store, which is teetering on the edge of an otherwise bankrupt strip mall. It's surrounded on one side by a clump of dilapidated structures that used to be homes, and on the other by a litter-strewn field. The package store is the strong shoulder on which the rest of the building and, evidently, the neighborhood itself, lean. It's been here as long as Wishbone can remember. He tells himself he'll grab a bottle, stop by the house for his fishing pole, and then head to the river where it's quiet and he can think, or not think.

As he steps out of the car, a girl wearing short-shorts and a halter-top saunters out from behind the store. She looks familiar, this girl. It's Katrina! Katrina, yes, the daughter of one of his mother's friends. Her daddy's in prison. Been there a long time. Dealing.

"Wishbone, where you been keeping yourself?" she says, muscles in her thighs vibrating with each high-heeled step. "You going out tonight?"

He tries to remember the last time he saw Katrina. She was just a little kid. Now look at her. Is she seventeen? Eighteen? "Just stopping here," he says.

"Let's party!"

"I gotta get on home," he says, fighting to keep his eyes off Katrina's long legs. Then he hears what sounds like an alarm clock.

Katrina pulls a cell phone from her back pocket. It's covered in a pink Hello Kitty case. "What?" she says into the phone, her tone sharp, her eyes cutting to the street.

He looks around at the empty stores, their bleak facades and blank, nameless doors, then back to Katrina and her pink phone, her smooth cheeks and jaw rolling the gum around in her mouth, grinding, grinding, now pausing to blow a short-lived bubble. As it bursts, Wishbone feels something pop inside himself, an abrupt snap in his sternum, his throat, his head. His eyes blur, then reset themselves, keen as ever.

He realizes he's still holding his phone. He slides it into his pocket, lets it go, while telling himself that Katrina is just a kid, a baby without her daddy to look out for her.

"I'll be home when I'm home!" Katrina says. She shoves the phone into her back pocket, rolls her eyes. "She never wants to let me go anywhere. I told her I'm sixteen. I can look after myself!" she says. Then she smiles. "So, we gonna party?"

"You need to get on home," he says, surprised by his response. It's as if he's listening to someone else utter these words and the sensation he feels, born of the sudden recognition of his responsibility, his inevitable, heavy responsibility, is completely foreign and new. Who does he think he is, anyway, giving orders to this young girl, to Katrina? Hasn't he done enough for the both of them? Who is he to talk?

He realizes he's undermining his own reputation, his own identity, twenty-two years in the making. Still, he pushes on, shouldering this new weight, heading now in a new direction, into a new territory, clinging to the thought of what should be.

"I'm sixteen. I don't have—"

"You gone get into trouble out here," Wishbone says. "Get in and I'll give you a ride."

"What? You gotta be my parent now?"

"Your daddy wouldn't go for you being out here."

"My daddy's in prison!"

"That's what I'm saying. Get in. I'll be right back," he says, stepping into the package store.

Inside, Cinco, the manager, says, "Happening, Wishbone? Bottle of scotch tonight?"

"No," he says, shaking his head, turning his attention now to a small wooden box on the opposite end of the counter. He takes one of the cigars and places it under his nose, and smiles. It smells sweeter than he anticipated. "Just one of these."

"Celebrating tonight?"

When he looks out the door, Katrina is sitting in the car, pink phone to her ear.

"Yeah, man," he says. "I tell you I'm gone be a daddy?"

8

Trophy Water

Flinging flies for trout isn't Denkelman's idea of fun. But somehow you've convinced him to forgo the golf course today and join you here on the White River in northern Arkansas for a morning of fly fishing. And because this has always been your idea of a great time, and because you want to be a good host, a generous ambassador to the sport, you spent three hours at the vise last night, tying him an assortment of your favorite patterns: scuds, sowbugs, pheasant tails, hare's-ear emergers, soft hackles, and midges. In the back of your mind, there is the possibility of Denkelman getting hooked on fly fishing, and if he does, he'll have some flies to get him started. This isn't likely, however. You tell yourself Denkelman lacks the necessary patience, and having no background or foundation in angling, he can't appreciate what it means to catch a trout on a fly rod. Besides, he's most at home on the golf course.

You've outfitted him with waders, a vest, and an old Thomas & Thomas rod with a beautiful medium action, while cautioning him that fly fishing isn't like dunking bait. But as Denkelman has never fished, this doesn't seem to register. Nor does he appear the least bit intimidated by what, to most outsiders, are the sport's mysterious intricacies.

Like casting.

"You've seen how far I can drive a golf ball," Denkelman says, stepping into the water, rings echoing across the smooth surface like his voice. "By noon, I bet I'll be able to cast across this river."

"Why would you do that when the fish are right here?" you ask. "Look, Denk," you say, pointing your fly rod at the water. "There's one right there."

"What can I say?" he says, stripping line off his reel. "Those who can, do."

"That remains to be seen." You tap the bib pocket on your waders, feeling the sleeve of Swisher Sweets and anticipating the smoke you'll have later. "Reel in about half that line. You don't need it."

"We can put some money on it," Denkelman says. "See who catches the most fish?"

"We're here on the river now," you say. "The point is to relax and enjoy yourself. Fly fishing's not a competitive sport."

"Or the biggest fish?" he adds.

"I'll show you how to catch big fish later," you say. "Right now you have to learn to cast." You remove your fly from the hook keeper and flip it out into the water. "Just focus on rolling the line, like this, and laying the fly upstream. Then mend and follow it down with the rod. That's all you have to do."

When he seems to understand this concept, you point Denkelman to your favorite pool, telling him to start at the head and slowly work his way downstream. "Don't worry if you don't catch one right away," you say. "It's taken me a long time to be able to come here and catch fish with confidence."

"We going to keep any to eat?"

"Gotta let them go, bro. This is trophy water. Catch-and-release."

Denkelman reels in his line and starts to head downstream, toward the pool. Now he turns back and looks at you. He's grinning. "Man, I gave up a good golfing day," he says. "I could be out there winning some jack today."

"After you catch a few of these trout you may want to sell those golf clubs."

"Yeah, right," he says. "I guess you wouldn't lose any more money, though, would you?"

Hearing this, your mind leaps back in years to a time when Denkelman was brand new at the office, a junior agent, and you were assigned to train him in the finer points of insurance. Even then he behaved as if he knew more than you, as if you were the new hire. Thinking about it now, you shake your head and laugh. It's strange, isn't it: the way time, many years spent together under the same company banner, building careers, allies in a common struggle, has a way of smoothing our sharp edges, our garish flaws, like these stones beneath your boots, polished smooth by eons of flowing water? Or maybe it doesn't do that at all. Maybe it only alleviates our aversion to them. You walk upstream toward the next pool, comforted by the thought of the river and the chilly fish-spirited air filling your nose. Spending so much time here over the years has shaped you, just as the current has carved the riverbed. How many times has it humbled you? Built you up? Offered you a salubrious antidote to work, middle age, city life? And how differently do you see the world for the hours, weeks, years you've spent, knee-deep in its essence, casting flies to the speckled jewels swimming these waters? More often that not, when you think of the White River you also think of yourself. By now, it's like the blood flowing through your veins. It sustains you. It's part of who you are.

"Don't catch them all," you say as you stumble upstream, the river rocks clinking beneath your boots, the noise radiating across the surface of the emerald-tinted river, sounding familiar, sounding hollow.

An hour later you glance downstream and see Denkelman whipping the five weight back and forth, throwing tailing loops and probably a wind-knotted leader. For a moment, you think about walking down and coaching him through a few fish. Then you remember the money you lost in that putting competition the last time he got you onto the golf course, and the ribbing you took. You decide to let him come to the realization on his own. The realization that fly fishing isn't as easy as it looks, and that sometimes we don't know as much as we think we do.

A little humility is good for all of us, you tell yourself as you tie on a scud fly and roll it out into the run before you, again and again. But again and again you come away with nothing.

After a while, you remove the scud and tie on a sowbug. When this doesn't work, you try a pheasant tail. And when even this fails to tighten your line you slide the little Wheatley box from your shirt pocket and select a soft hackle. And it's here you notice the two black-and-white zebra midges. You can't remember the last time you used them. You had intended to add them to Dink's box, but somehow you overlooked these tiny flies. The larger one is unweighted and understated, nothing more than a few wraps of thread on a hook. Simple. Practical. Effective. The other is even smaller. It features a glass bead, giving the fly a bulbous head, a flashy appearance, and reminding you of Denkelman. You laugh at the thought.

Thread midges, like these, were the flies you'd used years ago when you were new to fishing tailwater trout. You knew they caught fish. But at some point you'd reached a certain level in your progression as a fly fisherman where you realized that catching fish on these miniscule morsels was so easy that you considered using them beneath you. And because of this, you became adept at fishing more traditional flies, like dries.

Midges, you've told yourself over and over, are what you use to learn *how* to catch trout. It doesn't matter that at any time of year, at any point in the stream, there is some variation of the tiny two-winged insects available to the trout. It doesn't matter that midges catch fish on the hottest summer days, or in the most frigid part of winter. To you, midges are petty and insignificant—so insignificant that the trout have to constantly eat them in order to sustain themselves, so lacking they are of any substance. Any other angler would see the value in this. But not you. You consider them beginner's flies, like Woolly Buggers, probably because that's what these Ozark fly shops sell to the bobbing sports who drift down from the cities on weekends.

Shafts of light from the quickly rising sun behind the trees illuminate patches of the glassy and otherwise shaded water around you, where trout reveal themselves through their movements. As you cast, you picture their svelte bodies hovering along the current seams. Though you can't see them, you know they're here, camouflaged in this low light, hidden against the dark bottom, invisible until one drifts left or right to take some unseen wisp and the movement catching your eye and you studying the window framing this movement for several seconds, trying to spot this fish, other fish, before another flicker of motion somewhere else lures your attention away.

Splashing sounds distract you. Across the river, an old man in hip boots stands a few yards from shore, shin-deep, his back hunched, fly rod bowed under the weight of a leaping fish.

You take a few steps to your left and roll your fly upstream as you watch the old man net what appears to be a fourteen-inch brown, an average trout for this river. He removes the hook without lifting the fish from the water, his hand cradling the trout until it splashes away with the flick of its tail.

Now the old man looks your way and nods as he gathers his line to make another cast. "Grey midge," he offers. "Drifted right along the bottom."

"Thank you," you say, feeling somehow that this is your line, that you should be the one offering kindly advice.

You retrieve your fly and examine it to make sure it isn't fouled. Amid a growing sense of befuddlement, you study the fly in your fingers while mentally perusing the inventory of patterns inside the four fly boxes you've brought to the river. There is a certain security in having so many flies, a certain confidence in knowing you're prepared for any eventuality. One or more of these dozens of flies could work, could help the fish overcome their reluctance to eat, could change your luck, could change the day, could remind you again who you are and why you do this. But which one?

For a moment, you consider going to a midge. But it isn't the fly, you tell yourself. The problem is where it's drifting in the water column. It's not deep enough. You decide to add some weight.

As you crimp a BB-sized split shot onto your leader, more splashing sounds hook your ears and you look across the river but the old man is motionless and his fly rod under no strain as he concentrates on the water before him. Glancing downstream, you notice Denkelman is into a fish. He looks upstream as he plays the fish and you give him the thumbs up while telling yourself that what you need is not only more weight, but also a longer leader. A thinner leader. One made of fluorocarbon. Time for the 7X, you tell yourself as you pull a spool of the nearly invisible, gossamer line from your vest.

The sun has risen above the trees on the far bank and now illuminates the water in earnest, revealing dozens of trout all around you, while somewhere beyond, in the woods, a woodpecker hammers a tree, searching, searching, searching. For a moment, all is quiet except for the sounds of the current spilling around your legs, and again you wonder if you shouldn't try that midge, just to break the ice. It bothers you to think of fishing a midge, but what's worse is the thought of Denkelman showing you up. On *your* river. That would be like you schooling him on the golf course. And that's never going to happen.

Eventually, you give in and tie on the beaded zebra midge. And it works! On the *first cast!* Now, as you remove the diminutive fly from the little trout's mouth, you tell yourself that at least you aren't skunked, that now, at last, you can get down to business and concentrate on catching a real fish—and a big one. So you clip off the midge and gossamer tippet and replace them with heavier line and a meaty sculpin pattern. You might not catch as many fish this way, but you picture yourself hanging into one of the river's broad-backed behemoths and, after a protracted fight, lifting it from the water and saying, very casually, to any wide-eyed spectator within earshot, *Yeah, she's not bad.*

Catching big fish doesn't happen often, but every once in a while you get lucky.

Usually it's when you're fishing alone, like that day last December when you hauled in that big brown from the same pool Denkelman is fishing now. And like that time in the Florida Keys when you were casting to the channel edge on an incoming tide and you felt your fly stop dead in the water, and thinking you were hung on a piece of coral, and then the coral beginning to move slowly, steadily, straight out to deep water, and you, with an eight-weight bonefish rod in your hand, wondering how you were going to land whatever it was on the end of your line, and after a prolonged battle, your surprise at hauling in a permit, a heavy one, and the way its big black eye regarded you as you lifted it from the water, and later, the man at the tackle shop congratulating you and insisting that most of us fish all our lives and never catch a permit.

But you have and you wish Denkelman could have been there to see it instead of sitting back at work, inside that corner office with his name on the door, that corner office that should have been yours.

He can have that, you tell yourself. That's his business. Besides, you have a beautiful wife of almost thirty years, two healthy kids, a nice home. And fly fishing. This is the only sport you've pursued as an adult and you've done it for so long that it's difficult to imagine yourself doing anything else. Yes, Denkelman can have his golf and his BMW and that promotion, but you have fly fishing. This means something. You don't have to wave money around to enjoy yourself; you know better than that. You've always told yourself it's enough to enjoy the simple pleasures of a day on the river, casting flies to trout. This has always been its own reward, and still is. Isn't it?

The problem is, it's too late in the morning and the conditions too bright to reasonably expect to hang into a really big trout. And as you glance downstream, watching Denkelman release another fish, this fact begins to sting like a sharp hook through the skin.

Frustrated, you remove the sculpin and turn again to the zebra midge. But before you can attach the tiny fly to your leader, you fumble and drop it, and the fly, despite its flashy glass bead, disappears with the current. Gone. You can almost hear the tinny *tick* sound as the diminutive fly settles into the rocks on the river bottom somewhere downstream. You cringe, thinking about the trout that will sip it in. At least the miniscule hook will rust and fall out of the fish's lip or throat, you tell yourself. Or maybe the fly will never find its way out of the rocks. Maybe it will stay down there, unknown and forever unseen, and the river and fish none the worse for its presence, for your vanity.

Such are your thoughts as you tie the plain thread midge— your only other midge pattern—onto your tippet. And as before, the first cast produces an almost immediate tightening of your line. But it only gets so tight before you feel that sudden slackening that's always so sickening, and from the quick jolt you know the fly has parted ways with your tippet. You lift the line from the water. Seeing the bare tippet with no fly attached, you slap the line back down on the surface in frustration as your mind grapples with the one that got away.

At this point you reel in your line and then, on stiff legs, trudge from the cold river and head back to the truck, your neck hot, your feet frigid and numb. Here, you drop the tailgate and take a seat beside the ice chest where, in the shade of the tall pines, fly fishing suddenly seems a petty, meaningless sport and you a fool for pursuing it, a damned fool whose greatest accomplishments in angling now seem so arbitrary and insignificant. For a moment, fly fishing is strangely like an unfulfilled career, or a resume that will never read the way you want, despite the years and effort you've put into it.

Minutes pass. You think briefly of breaking your fly rod over your knee and slamming the splinters into the garbage can. You consider driving off and leaving Denkelman. For a moment, you fantasize about disappearing to some Central American country where you could sell coconut drinks in the mornings and fish and swim in the afternoons, living on whatever you catch.

Now you find the pack of Swishers in your bib pouch and suddenly things don't seem so bad.

A while later, cigar stub clamped between your teeth, you slide the old Wheatley box from your shirt pocket and inspect its contents. Except for a few errant flies, hastily pinned inside after your last fishing trip, the patterns are neatly arranged and ordered from the smallest pheasant tails and scuds at the top, to the larger wets and streamers along the bottom. There is something comforting in the orderly arrangement of these flies. There is something reassuring in knowing that every fly in the box is a product of your own vise and bobbin, in knowing that every wrap of thread and dubbing is yours, that each and every head is cemented and sealed. This means that you can count on each fly to hold up even after catching several fish. You can count on it. Even if other things are beyond your control.

With the flies, at least, it seems everything is as it should be.

You look up and glance down the path leading to the river, expecting to see Denkelman, a smug grin on his face. But the path is empty and all is silent except for the sounds of a passing car out on the road, the hammering of a woodpecker somewhere back in the trees, searching, searching, searching, its beak boring beneath the bark for the nourishment that'll sustain it.

In your mind you picture Denkelman out in the river, struggling to cast, his leader kinked and wind-knotted and yet, somehow, him hooking another trout and feeling the line tighten, the fly rod bend, the fish's weight, heavy and alive, and the anticipation and excitement of glimpsing it for the first time. And though part of you wants to throttle him, you're also happy for Denkelman. You've fished for so long you can't even remember what it's like not to fish. You've fished for so long you simply cannot recall catching your first trout. Still, as an angler, you know exactly how this feels. And because of this, because you've given this gift to Denkelman today, the opportunity to shake hands with one of God's most beautiful creatures, one that lives in a world completely different than our own but which is as perfectly suited to its environment as we are to ours, and maybe more so, and one that, thanks to state regulations for this section of blue-ribbon water and the typically benevolent fly fishing ethic in general, will get to fight again another day, you feel, just for an instant, the indescribable joy and satisfaction of that electric tug on the end of your line, the feel of a trout sliding across your palm and back home again, the scent of fish on your hands at the end of the day.

And then it's gone. The pungent cigar smoke curls into your nose, coating your clothes, clouding around your head and scattering the mosquitoes.

You remove one of the errant flies from the box and reinsert it into the row alongside others of the same size and color, gradually feeling more confident and reassured as each fly is returned to its proper position, where it should be, and where it will be, the next time you need it.

9

It Gets Under Your Skin

Uncle Billy says the minnows won't survive in the goldfish tank. He says the goldfish can live just about anywhere, but the minnows need cool water and lots of oxygen. I thought he was joking at first because I once had a goldfish. I kept him in a glass bowl in the kitchen. He did fine until I changed his water. Then he began to list to one side and swim around in circles like he couldn't find his way. I buried him in my backyard—my old backyard, where I used to live with my mom—and told myself I was through with fish. They're too hard to take care of. They might survive in your aquarium for a little while, but they'll never really thrive outside their natural environment.

So I didn't believe Uncle Billy, but you know, he's right. One night, I took a dip net and scooped some minnows, flipped them into the goldfish tank. A few days later I noticed they were floating belly up, dead. Goldfish were fine, though.

Right now, it's the minnows that are selling. A certain size of minnow. Uncle Billy says the walleye are biting up North and that's why fishermen want the six-pound minnows. I'm from the North—Chicago—but I've never seen a walleye. I don't care a thing for fish. And yet I live on a minnow farm in Oklahoma. But that's only because my mom went off on her trip to who knows where. I keep thinking she'll come back, but she's been gone almost two years. I hope she comes back. If not, protective custody might send me to Canada to live with Helen.

After my mom left, her sister, Helen, tried to get custody of me. Helen doesn't have any kids of her own. I was never around her much, but I know she's cranky because she and my mom used to argue on the phone. I also know that Helen lives with three cats in an apartment in Quebec City, and even if I liked cats, even if I wasn't allergic to them, that's not for me.

I may be out in the sticks, working my tail off in this heat, but at least I'm with Uncle Billy and Aunt Martha. And until my mom comes back, I'd much rather be here than in some tiny, cat-infested apartment with crabby Helen.

"The four pounders are too small," Uncle Billy says. He pronounces it as *pound*as, with the emphasis on the first syllable. Uncle Billy talks funny. Everybody talks funny down here. Real soft and slow. They stretch out their words like some do a dollar, like they're trying to squeeze out every last cent. "They for ice fishing," he says.

I've never been ice fishing, so I don't know about that, either.

What I do know is that the blue van wasn't here this morning, the one all the Mexicans ride in. It wasn't here when I came out after breakfast. Uncle Billy's got me, but I'm only one. And I don't want to spend my time chasing minnows. There are four or five Mexicans, usually. Sometimes, six or seven pile out of that van. The one who speaks good English always asks Uncle Billy if he can use a couple more men—brothers or cousins or friends. He says they're hard workers. He says they'll work until dark without stopping for dinner. I wish they'd come back.

Since they haven't, it's Uncle Billy and me, a seine net between us, dragging the muddy bottom of the finishing pond. I can feel the soft mud on my feet, oozing between my toes, and I can't stand it. It smells like fish and dirt and cow manure. I can't see the bottom, which worries me. Uncle Billy says there are snapping turtles in some of these ponds. He takes a spot near the bank, tells me to swing around wide and come back to him. "See the world and come back home," he says.

I step off the pattern, one slow, mucky step at a time, trying to keep my balance while the thick mud sucks at my ankles. Suddenly, the automatic feeder erupts and blasts me with a wave of high-protein fish feed. Shielding my eyes, listening to Uncle Billy laugh, I try to move forward, but I can't see where I'm going. The mud and the water are warm, but every few steps the mud feels softer and the water cooler. In these places I sink nearly to my knees. At one point, I go in a little deeper, trip, and fall in. Now I've got that earthy, fishy taste in my mouth, pieces of grit between my teeth. Feels like I'm biting down on sandpaper.

I'm glad Helen isn't here. If she was, if she could see me now, I'm sure she'd throw a fit and use this as evidence for why I should be up in Canada with her. But I'm not going to Canada. I'm thirteen. I can look after myself.

"Let's go back," Uncle Billy says. I grab my end of the net and move back to the bank, trying to keep myself from falling in again. "Them Mexicans are faster than you," he says, pronouncing it *Mez*kins. "They don't sink into that old mud so bad." I glance over and think that he's grinning at me, but it's only the cigar in his mouth making him look that way.

When I get back to the bank, I turn and try it again. I make a big U-shape with the net, like the upside-down shape of Uncle Billy's cap brim, then I bring it back to the bank, come back home. When I get there, we drag the net up the dike onto dry ground, where flies are buzzing around the cow piles. I still can't get used to the smell of cattle, but it's the heat that bothers me most. It's so hot down here that it feels like you're carrying around extra weight on your head and shoulders. Hotter than a heat stroke, Uncle Billy says.

That's when people faint from the heat.

In the water, when you get them up near the surface, the minnows look like a big dark cloud, their black backs straight and narrow, all facing the same way, calm and orderly. But things change once you take them out of the water. The net gets heavy, and the dark mass of minnows turns shiny and bright. The fish flip around in constant motion, flanks flickering in the sunlight, gills lifting and falling, bodies bending into so many thousands of silver question marks. Uncle Billy says this is when they're most vulnerable, when there's no water to support their weight. Plus, you know, they can't breathe out of water.

"I still don't know why they're called six-pound minnows," I say. "They look pretty small to me."

Uncle Billy just laughs. The cigar stub is wedged into the corner of his mouth, and I can hear him breathing. His shirttail is hanging out of his jeans, the bottom half wet and shaded deep-blue from the water, the top half dry and light blue, buttons open halfway down his brown, hairy chest. "Let's get them over to the tank," he says. "Get them some oxygen, let them settle in. Larry'll be here tomorrow."

With that, we hoist the net into a tub of water, which supports the fish until we can get them to the tanks. Uncle Billy drives the tractor and I sit on the trailer as we make our way to the open-sided pole barn, where a dozen or so concrete tanks are located. Here, we lift the minnows out of the tub and move them to one of the big tanks. The water inside is clean and clear, but looks black because of the shade from the roof. Holding either end of the net, we lower it into the black, bubbling water, then open it to release the fish into their temporary home. I peer into the black water, but all I can see is my reflection. The tank is only three feet deep, but it may as well be nine or eleven. You can't see the bottom. You don't know deep you'd sink.

The fishy smell is very strong here at the tanks. This is where the minnows are graded, separated, and finally loaded into the tank trucks for transport to their destinations. This batch we just brought in from the pond is headed to Larry's Bait and Tackle in Ely, Minnesota, tomorrow afternoon. Uncle Billy ships his minnows all over the country. He says as long as they have some oxygen along the way, they're fine. But you have to keep them out of the sun and give them lots of cool water, or they'll die on you.

He says the trotliners are the ones who buy the goldfish. Goldfish last a lot longer than minnows and do better on the hook. I'm not sure what trotlining is, but I think it's how the river people fish.

Raising my voice to be heard over the sound of the bubblers, which are buzzing from tank to tank the length of the building, oxygenating the water, giving life to the fish, I ask Uncle Billy where the Mexicans have gone.

"They haven't gone far," he says. He removes the cigar from his mouth, spits, looks out at the field in the distance. "Work and family are the only two things a Mexican has. They won't be gone long."

I get it. I used to have a family.

It is nearly noon and there is a haze from the heat hanging over the land and the ponds, making it look blurry in the distance. If you stare out there for a few seconds, the field looks like it's jumping, floundering around like a fish on land. These ponds are separated by miles of green dikes running the length and width of the field. You can't see them all from here because it's so flat. But Uncle Billy says, from the air, the ponds look like windowpanes, all square and neat and even. Too bad the water's so muddy you can't see through them.

Aunt Martha says that school starts in about a month. It seems too hot to be thinking about that, but down here in the Red River Valley it's hot even in September. I don't really want to think about starting school right now. Seems too far off. But I know summer has to end, and I've been thinking about going out for football.

"You gonna be a defensive end?" Uncle Billy says, crumbling a piece of cornbread into a glass. Once it's half-full with cornbread, he tops off the glass with buttermilk. This is his lunch, which he calls dinner, and which he eats with a teaspoon.

"Receiver," I tell him, stuffing the last of a peanut-butter sandwich into my mouth. "If they can get me the ball, I can do something with it."

Hearing myself, I sound pretty confident. I shouldn't be. The last time I played football I hurt my knee and had to spend the second half of the season on the bench. Coach said I needed to work on the physical aspect of my game, which really meant that I needed to put on some weight and get stronger. This was right before my mom left.

Mom and I used to have a lot of fun. But even then, I knew that she had things on her mind, things bothering her. Sometimes, during football games, I'd look up in the stands and see her sitting there, alone, and staring off into space. She came to all my games, even though she worked two jobs. And she always took me out for pizza afterwards. I love pizza.

"You ever thought about wrestling?" Uncle Billy asks. "You're a small fellow, but you wrestle other guys your same size. You gotta work hard to keep yourself in shape, keep in top condition. It's a very disciplined sport," he says. "I have a lot of respect for wrestlers, because they have to show up and make weight, or they don't compete."

Aunt Martha walks by, her gold bangle bracelets jingling on her arm as she pats Uncle Billy's stomach. "You wouldn't make the team, would you?"

He smiles, his mouth full of cornbread.

"No, it's football for me," I say, mixing myself a protein shake. "I'll get my chance one of these days."

Less than a week after the Mexicans disappeared, another group shows up at Uncle Billy's looking for work. Two men and a teenager step out of a rusty Ford truck. The teenager stays with the vehicle, while the older men approach Uncle Billy at the barn.

Their clothes look faded and dusty. One of the men has a scraggly beard with a cap tipped way back on his head. Their skin is brown enough that I can't decide if they're Indian or just white guys who have been out in the sun too long. Lifting an iron disc onto a bar, I watch them from the garage for a moment before lying back on the bench and gripping the bar.

After a few presses, I hear footsteps on the garage floor. The teenager has walked over from the truck.

"How much you lifting?" he says.

"Oh, I don't know. It's only a hundred," I tell him, trying to decide his age. He looks fourteen or fifteen. "Trying to warm up."

"How much can you lift?"

What a rude question, I think. What does it matter to you? Buzz off, and get your own weights. But what I say is, "I don't know. I haven't lifted in a while."

"Got any more weight?" he asks.

I point, and he walks across the garage, grabs another fifty-pound disc, and slides it onto the bar. I grab another, do likewise on the opposite side. Then he lies back on the bench and pushes, drops his hands to his chest, and pushes again, lifting the weights. He has thick arms and a barrel-shaped chest covered with a tattered, gray T-shirt. As he pushes, he exhales sharply, and I can smell that same sweet-and-sour scent that my old football coach's breath used to smell like when he would talk to us in the locker room or during timeouts. It's not the worst breath I've smelled, but it's not pleasant, either. He smells like he needs a shower, too.

After six or seven repetitions, he gets up. "I've jacked car axles heavier than that," he says, grinning. His teeth are very small for someone his size. They have little gaps between them, but they're all even. Then he removes a round can from his back pocket and opens it. It smells like rotten fish feed. He takes a pinch of the black dirt and stuffs it into his bottom lip. He spits, then offers me the can.

"That's okay," I say, wondering how he's not sick. If I put that stuff in my mouth, I think I'd vomit.

He laughs and spits again, leaving grainy, brown puddles on the garage floor. I don't know why he doesn't walk outside to do that.

Now he points to the weight bench and, with his bottom lip bulging, says, "Let's see what you got."

I get down on the bench, take a deep breath, and adjust my grip on the bar, over and over. Finally I push. Getting the bar up is no problem, as my arms are already nearly extended. But when I bring the bar down to my chest, I can't raise it. Pressure builds in my face. My eyes feel like they're bulging. And then nothing. He helps me get the bar off my chest, and I sit up.

"Thanks," I say. "Guess I need to work up to that."

"That's nothing," he says, then he spits. "Try jacking a car transmission with the fluid leaking out all over your face." With that, he leaves the garage and joins his elder companions near the truck. They climb in and start the emphysemic old engine. Even from this distance, I can smell the worn interior of the truck, which reeks of dust, sweat, and cigarette smoke. As they drive off, the teenager, his arm resting on the door, raises his finger in a lazy wave.

I run a broom across his spit marks, smearing them. Then I pour water over the stains to wash away the tobacco grains. I still can't believe he spat on the garage floor.

Across the driveway, at the barn, Uncle Billy is filling the tractor with fuel. I walk over.

"You gonna hire those guys?" I ask him.

"No, them river people wouldn't work out," he says. "They work long enough to collect a little bit, enough to buy them a bottle. Then they take off on you. They like to steal, too."

A few minutes later, he walks over to the truck and pulls out a .22 rifle. His eyes are focused on something in the distant field. "Cormorant," he says, steadying the rifle against one of the barn poles.

I've learned that the cormorant is sometimes called a "water turkey." And nobody likes them. They're medium-sized birds that eat fish. They stalk the edges of ponds, sometimes several of them, picking off the minnows. Cormorants are protected by the government, but that doesn't matter to Uncle Billy. He says they'll eat up your profits, and there are too many of them. Maybe so, but I wish he wouldn't shoot them. I hate killing, so I look off in another direction.

A few seconds later, I hear the crack of the .22, the *clink, clink, clink* of a spent cartridge bouncing off the concrete floor. It feels like a heavy blockage in my chest when he says, "He won't get any more fish."

With two-a-day practices starting soon, I tell myself it's time to get back into shape. Besides the fact that I like football, I figure, making the team will prove to everyone (especially Helen) that

I'm adjusting well to life down here. I received a letter from her the other day, asking me how I'm getting along, telling me her door is always open if I decide I want to move back to the city and "get out of the mud," as she put it. Some part of me appreciates her willingness to take me in, but she doesn't seem to understand that I'm not a little kid anymore. I can make my own decisions now and decide what I want to do with my life. Right now, this includes making the football team.

So, I've started lifting weights on Mondays, Wednesdays, and Fridays. On the days I don't lift, I run two or three miles. I'm never going to be a heavy, muscular guy, but if I can put on some weight and build my strength a little, I'll have a better shot at making the team. Size and durability are important to coaches.

I run all through the month of August, and it's hot. The air here in southern Oklahoma is heavy and humid, and your clothes stick to you pretty much anytime you go outside.

A few weeks before school starts, I go up to Lincoln High and enroll. In addition to my basic classes, I have to choose four electives. I decide on accounting for one of them. The enrollment counselor tells me it's all about organization—organizing your debits and credits and assets and liabilities. "Each one has it's own column, and as long as you keep the figures in the right column, you come out all right," she says.

Another class I enroll in is typing. I don't really care about typing, but the two girls in line ahead of me enroll in it, so I decide to do the same. They're both good-looking girls. They're showing each other pictures on their cell phones, and laughing. It reminds me of my mom. She used to take pictures of me. I wonder if she still has them, or if she ever looks at them.

I don't have my own phone, which is a little embarrassing. I would get one, but I don't want to ask Aunt Martha. They're expensive.

Sometimes I wonder if my mom would ever call me, if I had a cell phone. But I know she wouldn't. Uncle Billy and Aunt Martha have one, and she could reach me if she wanted. She knows their number.

I round out my schedule with French—I was told that mostly girls take French—and football.

On the way out of the school, just before I reach the door, I hear girls' voices, lots of them, and the sounds of tennis shoes squeaking on a wooden floor. I look into the gymnasium and see the cheerleaders practicing their drills. They're chanting and clapping and smiling. They look happy. I'm happy watching them. Then I hear someone behind me.

"Excuse me," says a girl in a T-shirt, shorts, and running shoes. She's older than me, obviously in high school, and very pretty. As she moves past me, into the gym, her scent reminds me of the city. Then she turns back. "Practice is closed. Unless you're with the photographer."

"I'm with the football team," I say. "I was just watching."

She raises her eyebrows and grins as she gives me a quick once-over. "You better start eating or they're going to run you over."

"I'm a receiver," I say.

"You'll still have to move along. Practice is closed," she says as she kicks the rubber stopper out from beneath the door. As the door closes in front of me, she says, "Have a good afternoon."

Football practice has already begun, and school is only a week away, when Uncle Billy tells me it's time to grade the fish. By now, I've all but forgotten the Mexicans, and I guess Uncle Billy has, too, because I've been helping him all summer. I don't really enjoy this, but I don't hate it, either. Besides, with school starting, I know I'll be spending less and less time around here. That's one good thing about school.

The goldfish are in a category of their own, so it's the minnows we have to grade. Walleye season must be very good for the anglers up North, because we get trucks in for the six-pound minnows several times a week.

"But they don't want the four pounders," Uncle Billy says.

"Why not?" I ask. "Won't they eat the smaller fish?"

At this, he stops what he's doing, removes the cigar from his mouth, and tells me, "Mark, some folks like a nice, big old steak. That's what they want to eat. Other folks like to eat hamburgers." Streams of sweat run down his cheeks, staining his shirt. He takes his cap off, pulls a handkerchief from his back pocket, and wipes his face dry. I notice a small area of blue stitching in one corner of the handkerchief, and for a moment, I wonder what it could be. Then I realize the stitching is Uncle Billy's initials.

He pulls his cap over his head. Then he folds the handkerchief and returns it to his back pocket. "You know, if it was me," he says, "I'd want a big old steak every time. I think most folks would choose steak if they could. But now that doesn't mean hamburgers don't have their place. Everything's got its place and purpose in this life. Even a hamburger. You know?"

"I think so," I say, though sometimes I wonder where my place is. It's not out here in the mud, but it's not back home in Chicago, either. All that's gone.

In an effort to separate the steaks from the hamburgers, we take an aluminum grate and place it into the minnow tank. The grate is nothing more than a series of parallel slats connected to a main bar, which serves as the handle. There is a very small space between each slat—just large enough to allow the smaller minnows to escape while trapping the larger fish.

We start at one end of the tank and slowly move the grate through the water until we're only a foot or so from the opposite end. Uncle Billy takes a piece of rebar and runs it through the handle, which allows us to rest the grate on the tank. Here, the trapped fish will remain until a truck arrives to take them to their destination.

We repeat this process with three additional tanks until Uncle Billy feels satisfied that we've segregated enough of the larger fish to fill the next order.

"Why do you call them six-pound minnows?" I ask him.

"A thousand minnows of this size will weigh six pounds," he says, biting on the cigar stub. "You take a thousand of the smaller fish, you only get four pounds. There's a big difference. But like I said, both have their places."

Sometimes I wonder if my mom will ever come back, and if she does, how different it will be. I know I'm a different person now, and it could never be the same as before. In bed at night, I can feel, deep down inside, that some small part of me, the old me, has died. Yet part of me feels more alive now than ever. Maybe it's the fresh air I breathe out here in the country. Maybe it's all the hard work I do. Or maybe people just get tired of things after a while, tired of who they are, tired of their lives, and they feel like their hearts have just decided to curl up and go to sleep. Maybe this is why they decide to move on, so they can find some part of the world where they fit in, where they feel alive.

Right after I moved down here, Aunt Martha thought I should see the school counselor. So, I spent the last month of seventh-grade visiting with Mr. Nidu twice a week. I don't know that it helped, really, but eventually I got to where I enjoyed listening to him speak. He's Indian—an Asian Indian—and he has a really strong accent. But Mr. Nidu is nice. He would speak to me as an adult, not as a student like my other teachers. He even gave me his home phone number and said to call him anytime I wanted to talk, but I never did.

Football has made the idea of going back to school a lot easier. There are three other guys going out for receiver, and one guy who plays sometimes at receiver and other times at tight end. Coach Mike likes him at tight end because he's big, and he can block. Fine with me. One less big guy to compete with. I don't have the height of the others, but I am pretty fast. Maybe I'll fit in as a slot receiver, run the short routes underneath.

Coach Mike calls the receivers his "fly guys." He says we need to be like flies. That is, we need to "fly," as in go really fast, but we also need to move around a lot, like flies do. Hope we don't get flattened like flies do. I just want to make the team and get some playing time. To do that, I need to show the coaches that I can get open, catch the ball, and take the hits. The first two are no problem, but taking the shots may be. I've been drinking a lot of protein shakes, trying to put on some weight. If I were only twenty pounds heavier, Coach Mike would make me a starter in a heartbeat.

One evening, when I get home from practice, Aunt Martha tells me a man from protective custody has been out to talk to her and Uncle Billy to ask them how I'm adjusting to life down here. I notice the glassy look in her eyes, and it makes me wonder if they could force me to leave here and go live with Helen in Canada. This worries me a little, but more than anything, it makes me mad. They're not going to tell me where to live. As far as I'm concerned, things are fine here and only getting better.

"You know I love you and Uncle Billy," I tell her, giving her a hug. "They're not going to tell me how to live."

"You're a sweet young man, Mark," she says, sniffling, her gold bracelets jingling as she dabs the corners of her eyes with a tissue. Aunt Martha wears lots of gold jewelry. It's bright and shiny against her brown skin. "We're so glad you're happy here. "

"I'm not moving to Canada."

"I know you're not, baby. Don't worry about anything. You're doing fine. We're proud of you."

"You know, I had a good practice today. I think I have a really great chance of making the team."

At this, Aunt Martha's eyes water, and she buries her nose in the tissue. Her tiny shoulders shake. "They said they were going to send someone to observe you at one of your practices. I wasn't going to mention it, but I think you should know."

"When?" I say, my chest feeling tight.

"They didn't say."

Now I'm determined to make the football team. I don't care about being a small guy. I don't care that I didn't grow up here in Oklahoma. I don't care about the oppressive heat. I'm going to show the custody people they're wasting their time.

"Well, they're going to see a first-string receiver at the top of his game," I say.

From the driveway comes the sound of tires crunching gravel and the low rumble of an engine. It's Chip, the driver for Larry's Bait and Tackle, who is making his third trip down this month to pick up minnows. It's Saturday morning, the sky overcast and low, and I'm helping Uncle Billy again, mostly because he's still without any other help right now. He doesn't mention anything about the visit from protective custody, and I decide not to bring it up. I'm just going to go about my business and try to show everyone that I'm happy and capable of living my own life. I'm not a damn kid anymore. Why can't the custody people just leave us alone?

"The fish still biting, are they?" Uncle Billy says.

Chip, climbing down from the tank truck, shakes his head. "Man, it's the best walleye season I can remember. One of our customers brought in a twenty-seven incher the other day he caught with one of your minnows."

"Hot damn!" Uncle Billy says, slapping his hands together. "I told you my prices doubled, didn't I?"

This morning we have three tanks fully segregated and stocked with the six-pound minnows, while the smaller fish have been moved to a single tank on the opposite side of the barn. I grab a thick hose and connect it to the valve on the first tank of big fish, while Chip fits the other end to the tank on his truck.

When it's all connected, the minnows and water are drained into the truck. While we wait for the first tank to drain, Uncle Billy and Chip shoot the breeze. I duck down and knock out ten push-ups. Already drenched in sweat, I rest a couple of minutes, then do ten more. A few minutes later, a sharp crack sound startles me.

"He was way the hell out there, Bill," Chip says. "I don't think I could've hit him, either."

When I hear this, I rejoice silently.

Aunt Martha doesn't like Chip, because she says he's rough around the edges. He has a couple of earrings in his left ear, a tattoo on his right arm, and a ponytail. I see where she gets that, but he's really a good guy. Uncle Billy even says so. Aunt Martha says she still doesn't want him in her house.

"Daddy spent twenty years in the air force," she says very matter-of-fact, right hand over her heart. "He'd of just *died* to see a grown man wearing an earring. Lord, have mercy."

I wonder what Helen would think if I had an earring and a tattoo. Would she still want me to come live with her? What would those custody people think? I can hear their report in my head: *He's a lost cause, lady. He's one of them now. Forget him.* Would they leave me alone?

We drain the second tank and begin on the third when a white truck pulls in off the road and approaches the barn very slowly. A couple of short, dark-skinned men with mustaches get out and wave. Chip and I finish up with the third tank, while Uncle Billy goes over to talk with the men. After several minutes, he returns to the barn.

"Did you get you some help?" Chip says.

"They offered to start right now. I told them to be here Monday morning at six and they'd have a job. These guys are hard workers. They just put their noses down and go. That's why I like Mexicans so much."

It's like a weight has been lifted from my shoulders; Uncle Billy has his help. Now, if I can just make the football team.

It is one week before our first game, and Coach Mike is just about to let us go from practice. I haven't been approached by anyone from protective custody, nor have I noticed anyone strange lurking around the practice field. Are they going to send someone out to watch me, like an NFL scout? I could really have some fun with that by telling the guys I'm being recruited. But they wouldn't believe me. I wouldn't believe me, either.

We've had a good week of practice, considering how badly we played in our last scrimmage. Since we don't have a running game, the other team keyed on our receivers, playing us man-to-man. They shut us down.

I didn't do so well, either. I caught a pass but got steamrolled by a big defensive end and had to be carried off the field. I watched the rest of the game from the sidelines, wishing I were four inches taller and twenty pounds heavier.

So, today, before letting us go, Coach Mike calls the team together for a huddle and asks how many of us know Kevin Truman. The Kevin Truman who got into three fights the first day of school last year. The Kevin Truman who was suspended the last three months of the previous school year for the same reason. That Kevin Truman. Coach Mike wants to know which one of us is going to get him to play tailback for our team.

There are snapping turtles in one of the finishing ponds. Uncle Billy doesn't know how they got in there, but, like the cormorants, they take their share of fish. Of course, he doesn't want them in there, and if not for the Mexican men he hired last week, it would be me out there getting my toes bitten off!

From the barn, I watch as the men seine the pond, moving slowly through the soft mud. I look for any movement in the top of the net that might indicate they've picked up something heavy, but I see nothing so far. If I were to go out with the Mexicans and net one of these turtles, is this something that protective custody would report back to Helen? I consider this for a minute until Uncle Billy slaps me on the shoulder.

"Mark, I finally found a use for these little minnows," he says.

"I thought they were for ice fishing."

"They are. But not this time of year. So, I got lucky and sold them to a chemical company in Houston. Every last one of them." I can't tell if he's grinning or if it's the cigar.

"Why does a chemical company want minnows?"

"They turn them loose in their outlets to find out if they're leaking chemicals. If the fish can survive, they figure they're all right. If they're leaking anything, why, they'll know it."

A few minutes later, Uncle Billy nods his head in the direction of the Mexicans out in the hot field. They are out of the water now, standing on the dike, and holding the net. It contains a large dark shape.

"Looks like they got them one," Uncle Billy says. "I told them they could have it if they caught one. They like to make soup out of them turtles."

"Turtle soup?" I say. "That sounds gross."

He laughs. "Depends how hungry you are."

The Tuesday before our first game I arrive late to practice and am ordered to run laps around the field. I'm only five minutes late, but Coach Mike tells me to start running. He says he'll tell me when to stop.

It's brutally hot outside, and even though I took a long drink from the water fountain before coming out here, my mouth and throat are parched. My head feels like a pressure cooker as I make my first lap around the field. Why am I not sweating much?

I notice a man sitting alone in the bleachers and observing our practice, a baseball cap on his head, sunglasses shielding his eyes. I'm fairly certain he's the one Aunt Martha was talking about, but I can't be sure. If Coach Mike hadn't ordered me to run laps, I think I might just walk over and tell him he's wasting his time, to go back to his office, and find someone else to harass. Seeing him makes me run harder, faster, even though I feel shaky and tired today. I guess it's because I started cold. But I'll warm up.

Then I pass the defense working out on one end of the field, the lineman pushing the skids, assistant coaches yelling for them to push harder, faster. Accounting is the reason I'm late, I think to myself. I'll admit, it's a boring class, and part of the reason is that they go to such lengths to make sure everything is in its own little column. This charge here, and that charge there.

Man, it's hot. I have to pass accounting, or I can't play football. I need a drink of water.

I round the opposite end zone and watch the other receivers going out for passes. I should be out there with them. If not for that stupid ledger assignment. Assets equal liabilities plus owner equity. Who cares?

Hey, isn't that the new guy? The new running back? The strong guy with the little teeth. He's on our team now. When is Coach Mike going to tell me to stop? I'm so thirsty.

But I'm cooling off. It's hot. It's darn hot, but I think I'm beginning to cool off. Beginning to. Beginning. Is *beginning* spelled with two g's and one n? Or is it spelled with one g and two n's? *Beginning*. Why did I have to take accounting? That counselor was right, but she didn't tell me the whole story. What's that girl's name in the first row, right side of the room? She might have been checking me out today.

I pass the bleachers and the strange man again, now no longer sweating, but feeling very hot, feeling the pressure of the heat boiling beneath my helmet, its weight on my shoulders. I keep running, watching Coach Mike to see his signal for me to stop, to go for a drink of water. Rounding a corner, I notice him standing and talking with one of the other coaches. Perfect occasion, I think to myself.

Occasion! That's another one! That's the other word I was thinking of. Another one that tricks me. Is it spelled with two c's and one s? What the heck does occasion, however you spell it, have to do with accounting? Or football?

God, it's hot! Does he even see me out here? Old Coach Mike. He even know I'm still out here running? What about the man in the bleachers? He see me? He see I can run, I can play?

First game coming up Friday night. Am I going to start? Is Coach Mike going to start me? Why does my heart feel this way? Why is my back all itchy now? Dry and itchy. Goal post flashing? What's his name? The new guy? Running back? Meanest kid in school?

Just keep running! Keep your balance. Keep that nice, smooth stride. The man in the bleachers is watching!

After passing out in practice, I wasn't sure I'd make the team. But when our best receiver, Sam Hightower, twisted his ankle the day before our first game, Coach Mike gave me a chance.

It's a good thing, because Uncle Billy, Aunt Martha, and I have a meeting with the custody people in a few days. Aunt Martha says it's no big deal. She says they just want to file a progress report. They want to see how I'm doing down here.

I keep telling myself that what I do out on the field tonight is more important than anything I could say in an interview.

We're down by five points with barely two minutes to go in the game when I catch a pass on a quick out pattern to gain five yards. The other team has shut down our running attack, and Coach Mike has sent me in as a distraction, hoping to spread the defense. It's a strategy we've worked on in practice. Coach Mike calls it the "bait and switch."

It's raining and I'm covered in mud. A plug of grass is wedged into my facemask, but I ignore it as we line up in the same formation for the next play.

Once again, I catch a short pass on a quick out pattern. I juke one defender, and another, then race down the sideline for a gain of eleven yards before I'm knocked out of bounds. I skid across the ground, my knee plowing a furrow in the soggy turf.

I feel like I'm flying. The crowd is roaring. The rain is hissing. The opposing coaches are yelling at their players.

We're running a high-tempo, no-huddle offense, and we line up the very same way on the next play. This time, however, Coach

Mike gives us the signal, and I know Kevin Truman, our new running back, is going to get the ball.

As I wait for the snap, the opposing coaches shout at their defense. "Watch the little guy!" they say. A moment later, another defender appears in front of me, his jersey, like mine, soiled and muddy.

Now I'm double-teamed, and I see a third player, one of the linebackers, glance over in my direction.

I lean forward just so, arms dangling, feet ready to spring off the grass and push me across the line of scrimmage. At the call of *Set!* my body freezes, muscles taught, my ears straining to hear the call over the noise of the crowd and rain as the clock winds down. For a second or two, I imagine Helen and the guy from protective custody sitting together in the stands, watching me, and waiting. But it's too late. I've already made the team.

Acknowledgments

Stories in this volume originally appeared in the following publications: "Second Chance," *The Ne'er-do-Well*; "Under the Bar," *The Heartland Review*; "Walleyed," *The Cleveland Review*; "Something to Hold On To," *Jelly Bucket*; and "It Gets Under Your Skin," *Louisiana Literature*. I wish to thank the editors of these journals for supporting my work, and I extend my gratitude to Robert Hand and the staff of Bowen Press for undertaking this project. Also, as some of these stories were years in the making, I'd like to thank the many people who have helped or encouraged or guided me along the way, including Richard Panek at Goddard College in Vermont; my colleagues in the inaugural class of the University of Central Oklahoma's MFA program in creative writing: Roy Giles, Paula Sophia Schonauer, John Goodine, Chase Dearinger, Noah Milligan, R. J. Woods, and Kevin Atkison. I'd like to thank Professor Susan Kates at the University of Oklahoma, Jonathan Starke, the Reverend Al Poteat, and Raymond Carver and Jack London, two of my literary heroes whose stories inspired me to write. Additionally, I extend my gratitude and respect to the proud few who've earned the right to wear the Marine Corps eagle, globe, and anchor—my old friends and fellow Leathernecks with whom I served, and those who continue to keep our nation safe today. Finally, I'm especially grateful to my wife, Ellen, and son, Jackson, for their love and support.

CPSIA information can be obtained
at www.ICGtesting.com
Printed in the USA
FSHW011548081020
74540FS